DOCT

DALEK

THE CHANGING FACE OF DOCTOR WHO

The cover illustration of this book portrays the Ninth DOCTOR WHO, whose appearance later changed when he absorbed the time vortex to save the life of his best friend, Rose.

DOCTOR WHO

DALEK

Based on the BBC television adventure
Dalek by Robert Shearman

ROBERT SHEARMAN

BBC
BOOKS

BBC Books, an imprint of Ebury Publishing
20 Vauxhall Bridge Road,
London SW1V 2SA

BBC Books is part of the Penguin Random House group of companies
whose addresses can be found at global.penguinrandomhouse.com

Penguin Random House UK

Doctor Who is a BBC Wales production for BBC One.
Executive producers: Chris Chibnall and Matt Strevens

First published by BBC Books in 2021

www.penguin.co.uk

A CIP catalogue record for this book is available from the British Library

ISBN 9781785945038

Editorial Director: Albert DePetrillo
Project Editor: Steve Cole
Cover design: Two Associates
Cover illustration: Anthony Dry
Production: Sian Pratley

Typeset in 11.4/14.6 pt Adobe Caslon Pro
by Integra Software Services Pvt. Ltd, Pondicherry

Printed and bound in Great Britain by Clays Ltd, Elcograf S.p.A.

The authorised representative in the EEA is Penguin Random House Ireland,
Morrison Chambers, 32 Nassau Street, Dublin D02 YH68.

Penguin Random House is committed to a sustainable future for
our business, our readers and our planet. This book is made
from Forest Stewardship Council® certified paper.

FSC www.fsc.org MIX Paper from responsible sources FSC® C018179

To Russell, Mark, Paul and Steven – look what we started . . . !

And to the original Owen Bywater,
the friend at school who got me into Doctor Who *in the first place.*
It's all his fault.

And I'd like to thank
Alex Romeo, Sam Durneen, Stuart Hardy and Alex North.

Prologue

It begins, as it so often does, with a boy standing on a hill.

It is a little hill, for he is only a little boy. And from the top of it he can see the entire world stretched out before him – lush rolling fields, and thick-trunked trees, and deep lakes, and … No.

No, it is a *big* hill, the very biggest the boy can imagine. (It shoots up higher and higher, how high can it possibly go?) On the peak the boy feels as if he's scratching the sky. He's not sure how he feels about that. Maybe he begins to feel just a bit afraid.

We don't want the boy to be afraid. Not just yet. So:

A boy stands on a medium-sized, perfectly unthreatening hill, and he is happy.

He can see for miles. The rolling fields, yes, and the thick-trunked trees, and – there is something missing. What is it? The boy suddenly realises – there are no people.

There is no one anywhere, not in any direction, no matter how hard he looks. He is entirely alone.

The boy wonders whether this should bother him, and then decides that it doesn't. No one – not even his parents! – but it's fine. It's good. The boy then wonders why he can't remember his parents, whether he even has parents. Should this bother him too? He's not sure.

He'll put it aside for a while. He'll work that one out later.

The peace of it. The utter, unbroken tranquillity – and all around him, fields (rolling), trees (thick), lakes (deep), and yes, up above too, that rich blue cloudless sky, just look at it, doesn't it make your head spin? Why, it could go on forever.

The boy revels in it. The freedom. And more than that, the *isolation*. And from deep within a thought suddenly occurs to him.

Enjoy this while you can. Because very soon the others will come. So many others, you have no idea! There'll be so many, and they'll blot out the sky, they'll block your view of the fields and the trees and the lakes. They'll fill in every last bit of space, and you'll never, ever be on your own again.

The monsters are coming.

The boy pushes these thoughts away, he tucks them into the part of his mind that's still worrying why he can't recall whether he has parents or not, and what his own name is, and isn't he actually in pain, isn't there some terrible pain he's refusing to acknowledge?

The sky is vast and empty, and is broken only by a kite, and then the boy realises with delighted surprise that it's *his* kite, and he's the one holding the string.

There doesn't seem to be any wind. Not so much as the hint of a breeze that could disturb the calm of the scene. But the kite darts about the sky anyway, dipping this way and that, as if it's an overexcited child that can't keep still, as if the kite was a little child and this boy was a big grown-up looking after him. It makes the little boy laugh.

Its wings are fragile, and only the little boy can protect it, and he *will* protect it, it's his mission.

The monsters are coming, they're getting closer, and once they're here you'll never be alone again.

The boy loves the pull of the kite in his hands. That he's got it under control. That he's the one giving orders.

The monsters.

And from behind a cloud he didn't even realise was there, the sun breaks through, and it's warm and it's beautiful and it fills the world.

The boy stretches out his hand towards it, he wants to touch it.

The kite is loose, he's lost the kite! The boy doesn't care.

Straining high to reach the sun. On his tippy-toes now, the little boy with his little arms and his little fingers itching for that warmth.

It's a moment of pure joy. This boy, this nothing boy, without a name or family (or future), daring to bask in the sunlight. And the green of the grass and the brown of the trees and the blue of the sky, and all the colours, and all the smells, and so many *ideas*, he has so many ideas, and things he wants to do and say and feel.

The monsters say, *These ideas are not for you.*

His arm is too heavy, it drops hard to his side. No, his whole body is too heavy, he cannot move.

The world, suddenly, is too heavy.

He watches helpless as the kite crashes to the ground. Too fast, too hard, those fragile wings shatter on impact.

The boy manages to say one word – 'No' – and it doesn't sound like the voice of a boy, it's already harsh and grating, and so so old, and so so tired.

Even the sky is too heavy, he can feel the vast weight of it as it bears down upon him.

As it contorts and tapers into an enormous finger. As it presses down hard, as it squashes him deep into the hill.

The boy is no longer there, and then the hill is no longer there, there is only that weighty murdering sky, and then the sky is no longer there, it's gone, it's gone. This world has been snatched away, it's gone forever.

The monsters are here. Never forget what you cannot be. And never forget what you truly are.

1

The creature was in constant pain, but it had stopped caring years ago.

It dimly remembered caring. Sometimes it would struggle to recall what that felt like, to care – it had felt good, hadn't it? But the memory was too weak to grasp on to. It was one of the things that had fallen away, and was lost. Like so many of the other things. Power. Pride. Point.

The creature was not afraid to die. Not if dying was part of its mission. But the problem was exactly that, it couldn't be sure. Some days it believed it entirely, that death was its sole purpose now, and the realisation washed over like cool relief. But then the doubts would get in. What if instead its purpose was to stay alive? Was that possible? It was surely possible. What if survival, really, was now its only function? So, then, survive. Live on. No matter how hard the suffering.

And so that's how it had existed all these years. Caught between the not-quite living and the not-yet dying. Keeping its options open, waiting for new information that would help determine which was better. The agony of the torture no worse than the agony of the indecision.

It was a wonder it hadn't driven the creature mad.

But it wasn't mad. Not yet. Not quite.

The human is here again. The one with the drill.

Some days the creature hates the human. That feels right, it is good to have hatred for the enemy.

But hatred makes his nerves come alive, when it is usually easier to hide within the numb. And besides, the creature knows that the man is just fulfilling its purpose. Its purpose is to make the creature's life unendurable. And although the man is failing – because the creature *is* enduring it, it *is* – having a purpose is still something the creature can respect.

Better the human with the drill than the other humans – the ones who come in to clean away the bloodstains on the floor, and never dare to look at it. Better him, than the man who comes to inspect, and to plead for it to talk, to beg.

The creature hates that man in particular, and cannot help it, no matter that the effort of such hating sets its nerves on fire.

The human with the drill is here again, and the creature knows that the pain is about to increase tenfold, and there's nothing it can do about it. And it envies its torturer a little, not for the ability to inflict pain, but that it sets about its task so thoroughly.

And it's true, the creature envies that ability to inflict pain as well. To be able to cause suffering again! That would be good.

Its scream takes even the creature by surprise.

It has been so many years since it made a sound that the creature was no longer even sure that it could. It had begun to wonder whether its speaking parts had atrophied. It wondered whether, if it were ever required to speak again, it would quite remember how to do it.

It hasn't spoken because speaking is what the humans wanted it to do. And it hadn't made so much as a sound while they tortured it, because that gave the creature some small sense of satisfaction.

But now it is screaming. The scream is shrill and loud, and oh so anguished.

The human has penetrated another section of the outer casing, and is cutting into real flesh. It is agony, of course, but that is nothing new – the creature doesn't know why this latest atrocity in particular causes it to cry out, to break the silence of decades.

Maybe it isn't even the creature's choice. Maybe the man has cut into one of the defence mechanisms. Maybe the scream is a purely involuntary action.

Oh, it feels good to scream.

It feels good to cry out at the world, at the injustice and cruelty of it, and try to shatter them with its voice.

The creature sees that the human is recoiling. It is too loud for him. He has dropped the drill, clamping his hands desperately over his ears. Good. The creature is inflicting pain on him this time. *Good.*

And the scream is like a sharp spike. It drives upwards through the roof of the cell, it drives through half a mile of concrete until it reaches the surface and the desert above. And then it just keeps driving, up from this disgusting planet that has trapped him, up into the outer reaches of space.

Up, to find out whether anyone in the universe can care.

The creature knows that now it has been broken, there will never be silence again. But there could be a strength to that too. It will make that a strength.

It stops screaming. And the echoes ring around the walls as the human with the drill stumbles to his feet.

He is hurting. He is smiling too.

'Good boy,' he says to the creature. He sounds almost affectionate, he sounds *proud*. 'That's a start. Now, let's see what else you can do.'

2

Rose Tyler hadn't been travelling with the Doctor long, but already she thought she knew him better than she'd ever known anyone.

Sometimes this worried her. When they were apart, sheer common sense would speak up, and tell her that the whole situation was ludicrous. She didn't know him at all. How could she? With all the stuff he had seen and done, with the hundreds of years he had lived. And she was this 19-year-old girl from Peckham, and she'd got four GCSEs, and she'd worked in a shop. How could she ever think she *understood* the Doctor? That she could ever do more than scratch the surface?

But then, when she was actually with him – oh, it was different. Then she couldn't doubt it at all. He looked at her in a way no one had really ever done before: as if she were the single most interesting thing to be found in the entire universe, and he was fascinated by her. And they could talk – they could talk for hours without stopping! – they could talk about anything! So that's exactly what they did. She was never bored in his company, and somehow, wonderfully, he made her feel he was never bored in hers. The universe was incomprehensibly vast, but they weren't just tiny irrelevant specks against the scale of it – they were the Doctor and Rose, and they were vast and important too. The universe was *theirs* – and all they had to do was seize hold of it together.

She *did* know the Doctor better than she'd known anyone. And at the same time, she would only ever know a fraction of him, and that was what was so exciting, and so scary. At 16 she'd started a misguided relationship with Jimmy Stone, and he'd looked the part, he'd got a job and drove a moped. She'd thought she could spend a lifetime getting to know him; they'd begun dating on Saturday, and by that Thursday night watching the football in that pub in Vauxhall she'd realised she'd run out of things to learn. She'd drunk deep from an especially shallow glass.

When she'd met the Doctor he'd seemed weighed down by some terrible tragedy. She only knew a little of it, even now – he didn't like to talk about it. He was the last of his own people, a race called the Time Lords, the only survivor of a great war. He'd admitted that for years he'd been travelling the universe without care, seeing where the TARDIS would randomly take him. Doing his best for the people he met there, but never with any real sense of purpose. But he was happier now. He'd laugh. He'd tell jokes. They weren't very good jokes, but he would tell them! And sometimes he'd beam a smile that could charm the cosmos. He told Rose that he had found that purpose at last. He was going to show her *everything*. All the strange wonders of an infinite number of worlds, the wonders he had for so long taken for granted. He would see the universe anew through her eyes.

Rose didn't dare think she was responsible for his recovery, but she had helped him, surely? She knew she had. And so they explored the universe – and it's true, most of the time things went badly wrong, and they were plunged into terrible danger. But Rose didn't mind. The good times or the bad – what did it matter, so long as they were facing them together?

They were in the TARDIS now, his impossibly sized spaceship locked within a small blue police box that could take them everywhere and everywhen. The Doctor was in one of his ebullient moods, which meant he was practically dancing around the console as he operated the controls, and he was talking clever things nineteen to the dozen in order to impress her. And Rose loved him like this – but it always worried her too, as if he were trying a little too hard to be happy, as if he were pushing something away.

'There's a pleasure planet out on the Sydonian rim,' the Doctor was saying. 'And I thought, really, a whole planet for pleasure? A planet's a big place. That seems like a dare.'

Rose laughed. 'I could put up with a bit of pleasure.'

'Well, hold tight, Rose, because you're about to get 12 whole continents' full.' The Doctor grinned.

And then froze. He clasped his hands to his ears, his mouth gaped in surprise and pain.

Then Rose heard it too. The sound piercing through the TARDIS – loud, shrill, desperate. It filled her head. 'What is it?' she cried.

'Distress signal,' the Doctor said. 'Sent out on every wavelength, it's extraordinary.' He'd broken out of his paralysis, he was flicking switches and pulling levers at the console with ever more urgency. 'Trying to get a lock on it.'

Rose felt the TARDIS lurch as it changed course, and then the bottom seemed to fall out of the world – they were plummeting through space, downwards, hard and fast. And just as she was certain they would crash to the ground, the ship settled and the sound was gone.

'We're here,' said the Doctor. 'Come on!' And without even looking back he had opened the doors and he was out, striding into the unknown.

Rose chased after him. Good times, bad – so long as they were together.

'Where are we?'

'Earth. About half a mile beneath the Utah desert.'

'And when?'

'A few years into the future. I'll find a light.' She heard him move away. Her eyes began to adjust to the darkness. She dared take a few steps forward.

And then, there was light – right in front of her eyes, dazzling her, half blinding. A square of light, and in the centre of it was a skull. The skull was looking straight at her, out of two cavernous eye sockets – and Rose knew in an instant that it leered with utter hatred. It was dead, wasn't it? It was dead, and it wanted her dead too. Its head the size of a man's, but it was *wrong* – the forehead was too warped, and its mouth was too large, and its teeth, it had far too many teeth. It was too alien. It was dead, she knew it was dead, and yet it was lunging at her out of the dark.

She heard the Doctor call behind her. 'Rose! It's all right!' And then the rest of the room lit up all around her, he had found the light switch. She could see the skull properly. It was in a display case.

'Blimey,' said Rose. Trying to get her heart rate back to normal. Trying not to sound scared. 'We're in a museum. An alien museum.' She looked around her, and she saw the room was huge, glass cases lining walkways on all sides, stretching on as far as she could see. 'You're sure this is Earth?'

The Doctor was walking down and peering into the cases; each time he came close they would light up to show their contents more clearly. 'Yeah, Earth all right. Nowhere else in the universe has such a mania for sticking dead things behind glass.' He sounded amused. Her panic by now had been dismissed and forgotten.

For a second Rose felt annoyed, and then decided not to be. She caught him up. 'Hey, that's a bit of Slitheen,' she said. 'It's a Slitheen's arm!'

'Stuffed,' said the Doctor. 'Look at all this. Chunks of meteorite. Moon dust. That's the milometer from the Roswell spaceship.'

'Could that be where the signal came from?'

'No, it's dead. That signal was alive. Calling out for help.' The Doctor frowned. 'Most of this stuff is rubbish. But it's expensive rubbish. To have amassed this lot, it'll have cost a fortune.'

'So the owner is rich,' said Rose. 'What else?'

'Who sticks a museum half a mile underground?' said the Doctor. 'Hidden from the rest of the world? Someone with a lot of secrets. I think we should tread carefully.'

And that's when they heard the signal again.

Louder now, and more desperate – and one thing was finally clear, it wasn't simply a distress signal, it was a cry of pain. The Doctor was running towards the scream, and Rose was struggling to keep up – she thought, *So this is treading carefully is it?* Out of the room and down a corridor, and then banging hard upon a heavy metal door.

'Let me in!' the Doctor shouted. He aimed his sonic screwdriver at the door – it clanked open. The door had muffled the sound somewhat; now the scream was unbearable.

There were two guards in the room, each wearing protective ear covers. They were so surprised to see the Doctor and Rose that it took them a good few seconds to remember to point their guns at them.

Henry Van Statten had decided to decorate his main office with a portrait of Henry Van Statten. It was not a good portrait. He knew it was not a good portrait. He knew it, because he had commissioned a series of the world's most respected artists to paint the portrait, and each time he had had to reject what they had done because it *was* good. 'But what you are asking for,' one Turner Prize-winning artist had tried to explain, 'is entirely crass. You cannot expect creative minds of my calibre to produce something so culturally sterile, just because you have the money to pay for it.' But that is exactly what Henry Van Statten *did* expect. And he got what he wanted in the end, just as he always did – a highly praised Argentinian sacrificed his integrity and at last produced a picture that Van Statten found acceptable. It was awful and garish, and the Argentine had done it ironically, Van Statten could see that, Henry Van Statten was no fool. He saw how the artist must have sneered during the composition. But Van Statten didn't mind the sneering. He was used to sneering. He liked it.

Van Statten didn't know much about art, but he knew what he liked. And what he especially liked was a giant form of himself spread over an entire back wall, wearing a facial expression he chose to think was both authoritarian and condescendingly benevolent. He looked more robust, less dainty. There was emphasis to his bright, fierce eyes; the beard was trimmer; the double chins had been smoothed over.

Most of the time Van Statten loved the portrait. On bad days he feared it a little, and worried that the picture was more impressive than he was. And that was when he would consciously try to ape his own enlarged image. Rest his chin upon his hand in contemplative calm. Sit up straight. Make his eyes do that bright fierce thing the artist had depicted so well.

He hadn't been too alarmed when he'd heard there were intruders in the base. He had even allowed himself to be amused when they had demanded to see him – demanded indeed! But from the moment they were marched at gunpoint into his office, Van Statten felt curiously nervous, and the urge to imitate his portrait came upon him. He didn't know why he felt nervous; it was very irritating. He decided he would ignore them for a while, pretend that his very presence hadn't ruffled him at all. (Because someone breaking through all his security and making it as far down as the 53rd floor – didn't he have the right to be a little worried?) No, he would be nonchalant. Unimpressed. Smooth as the chins in the portrait behind him.

He stole a look at the intruders anyway, just a glance, so they wouldn't notice. One was a girl, he discounted her immediately. But the man was of interest – casually dressed in a leather jacket, a big grin upon his face. Exuding a confidence he had absolutely no right to have. Was that infuriating? Yes, that was infuriating. Was it intriguing too? Yes. So, good – Henry Van Statten liked to be intrigued.

'Sir, the prisoners,' announced some guard or another.

'They can wait,' said Henry Van Statten.

The portrait excepted, the rest of Van Statten's office was grey and functional. A bank of computer screens studded around the walls showed video images of the base. The desk was cold and spare; a child's telescope stood incongruously upon it.

Van Statten was flanked by Goddard, his second in command, and she didn't look worried; he thought she really ought to look a little worried, if only for what this security breach might mean for her job. The guards holding the intruders at gunpoint didn't look worried. At least the English kid he'd put in charge of curating his collection looked worried. But then, the kid always did, he never stopped squirming.

'All right,' he said to the kid. 'Show me my latest toys.'

'There's this piece here,' squirmed the boy, in that accent Van Statten never stopped finding funny. He passed over an ugly misshapen lump of metal. 'Won it at auction for 80 thousand dollars.'

Van Statten wished the boy had chosen something that had cost a great deal more. Something that might have impressed the intruder. He could almost sense him smirk. 'Yes, yes,' he said. 'But what does it do?'

The kid cleared his throat. 'Right. Well, you see those little tubes on the side? I think they must be to channel something. Fuel, perhaps? So, it's part of a spaceship engine?'

'I really wouldn't hold it like that.' The intruder's voice was low and serious.

Everyone in the room froze.

Van Statten felt the metal object in his hand; suddenly it felt properly alien, properly unknown. He felt his heart beat faster. Was he frightened, he wondered? No. No, he was excited.

The boy asked quietly, 'Is it dangerous?'

'No,' said the intruder. 'It just looks silly.' And he grinned, and he reached out his hand to take it.

Immediately the guards cocked their guns. Van Statten waved them down. Slowly, deliberately, and with an expression he hoped was every bit as condescendingly benevolent as his portrait suggested, he gave the alien object to the intruder.

'It manipulates atoms, makes the very air vibrate.' The man began to stroke at the metal gently, even lovingly. 'You just need to be delicate.' And soon a series of notes came out of the tubes – deep, and rich, and beautiful.

Van Statten was fascinated, all trace of his nonchalance was cast aside. 'It's a musical instrument,' he breathed.

The man smiled at it affectionately as the tune played on. 'And it's a long way from home.'

'Give it to me,' said Van Statten. 'I want to have a go.' So the man handed it back. Van Statten rubbed his fingers and thumbs hard over the surface. The only sounds he could coax from it were harsh and discordant.

'I did say delicate,' the man reminded him gently, and Van Statten looked up at him and glared – the man was mocking him, no – even worse – he was being *sympathetic*. 'It reacts to the smallest fingerprint. It needs precision,' and now Van Statten's cheeks were burning, and he hated this musical instrument, he hated it. If he couldn't master it in a moment he didn't want it at all – and then, just as he was about to give up and hurl it across the room, something sweet and melodic dribbled out in spite of itself.

Van Statten couldn't help it. He laughed with delight.

'You've got the knack,' said the man.

'It's better than what you did, isn't it?'

'You're quite the expert,' said the man.

And Van Statten beamed up at him in childlike pride – and saw that he really was being mocked after all.

He threw the instrument away. And he felt a thrill of pleasure to see the disappointment flush across the intruder's face. 'And now,' said Van Statten, 'you can tell me exactly who you are.'

'I'm the Doctor. Who are you?'

'Like you don't know. Here we are, hidden away underground with the most valuable collection of extraterrestrial artefacts in the world. And you just stumbled in by mistake.'

The Doctor didn't even have the decency to get flustered. 'Yeah, that pretty much sums me up.'

And for a moment Van Statten didn't know what to do. So he decided to use a time-honoured technique that kept his employees on their toes. He would change from urbane man of charm to raging monster. Losing his temper was always a last resort, but it never failed to cow them into submission – he'd show the Doctor how unpredictable he could be, how dangerous. He suddenly shouted, straight into the Doctor's face, 'Tell me how you got in!'

The Doctor didn't look cowed. If anything, he looked just a little embarrassed. The most he did was to raise one eyebrow, just a little.

And now Van Statten was worried everyone in the room would start laughing at him, that he'd have to start shouting at them too.

Goddard broke the awkward silence by giving Van Statten's name.

'And who's he, when he's at home?' The accomplice had spoken up. Van Statten had half-forgotten there even was an accomplice – he didn't tend to notice girls very often.

'Mr Van Statten is the head of Geocomtex, the largest telecommunications corporation in the world. He owns the internet.'

The accomplice wasn't impressed either; no one was impressed by Henry Van Statten today. 'Don't be stupid,' she said. 'No one owns the internet.'

So he closed his eyes and concentrated on the portrait: *smooth*, he thought, *smooth*. When he opened them he was smiling and languid, he was once more in charge. 'And let's just keep the world thinking that, right? You're English! I do so love the English. They sound so commanding, without actually having any power. Hey, English kid, we've got you a girlfriend to play with.' Neither the girl nor the boy seemed especially taken by the idea; Van Statten didn't care.

The Doctor said, 'It's an impressive collection, Van Statten. Though you should know you're displaying most of it upside down.'

'You claim greater expertise?'

'Oh, I never need to *claim*,' said the Doctor. 'I know how good I am. And what I'm interested in is the part of your collection that screams.' His voice was gentle. His eyes hard.

‘We caught you right by the Cage. It contains my one living specimen.’

‘And what is that?’

‘As if you don’t know.’

‘Show me.’

‘You want to see it?’

‘Blimey,’ said the girl, and she rolled her eyes. ‘You can practically smell the testosterone.’ And the guards laughed, they dared to laugh, and no one had laughed without permission in years.

‘Right,’ said Van Statten. ‘Right.’ Smoothness wasn’t enough, the fierce eyes weren’t enough, he would have to assert himself properly, starting right now. And he began to snap orders, as fast as he could think. ‘Goddard, inform the Cage we’re heading down. You, English kid. Take the girl, go and canoodle and spoon, whatever it is you English do. Maybe she’s an expert too, I’ll give her your job, let’s see, shall we? And as for you …’ He turned to the Doctor, and the Doctor just stared back at him, and no one had done that to Van Statten for such a very long while. ‘You, Doctor with no name. Come and meet my pet.’

3

The two guards posted to the Cage were called Bywater and Klein. Bywater was a big, gruff man from Chicago, Klein a petite Israeli woman who never spoke. They had absolutely nothing in common, but because neither of them had made even the slightest attempt to get to know each other, they had never found out how truly incompatible they were. Not as friends, not as colleagues – not even as human beings. In a funny way, their complete lack of curiosity had saved them – since they were unaware of how much they naturally would have disliked each other, they actually got on reasonably well. It was a boring job guarding the Cage. During their shifts they sat by side in silence, shared the newspaper each morning, and would take it in turns to make the other coffee.

It might be thought that they had been paired deliberately as comic contrast. But they hadn't. Van Statten didn't have that sort of sense of humour. And now as he swept into the Cage operations room, they both snapped to attention and saluted. They knew that their boss wouldn't acknowledge them, that he probably wouldn't even notice they were there – but it was the correct form of the thing. If they were surprised that he'd brought the intruder with them they didn't show it. They were paid not to be surprised.

'I hope you appreciate my specimen, Doctor,' said Van Statten. 'I will be disappointed if you don't. Whenever I have a bad day, all I need to do is pop down and visit him. He's done more for me than three wives and fifteen therapists.'

'But what is it?'

'We do keep asking, but there's the thing. It just doesn't want to tell us.' From behind a heavy metal door emerged a man in an orange protective suit. 'This is Simmons, and his job is to encourage it to stop sulking.'

Simmons pulled off a head mask. 'I've had to take the power down. The Metaltron is resting.'

'I'm quite sure,' said Van Statten crisply, 'the Metaltron will be too excited to rest when it sees the brand new expert we have visiting.'

'Metaltron?' said the Doctor. 'What, really?'

'We had to call it something,' said Van Statten. 'Good, isn't it? Though I'd like to find out what it's really called. And then I can see which name I prefer.'

Simmons offered the Doctor a pair of thick gloves. 'If you're going in there, you'll need these. The last guy who touched it burst into flames.'

'Well,' said the Doctor, 'I won't touch it then.'

'Go ahead, Doctor. Enter the Cage.' Van Statten smiled. 'And impress me.'

The Doctor smiled back, just long enough to leave Van Statten in no doubt how much impressing him was his express priority. He turned to the darkened Cage. He took a breath. He stepped inside. The door was closed fast behind him.

Van Statten stared up at the monitor screen greedily. 'Keep it locked until we get a result.'

The first thing the Doctor noticed was the smell. Hot metal, it was acrid, it burned at his throat. And there was a sound to accompany it – a flat sizzling, like a dying wasp.

He couldn't see anything yet. 'Hello?' he called out. It was too dark, and too *warm* too, that was the burning – with all his other senses dulled it began to overwhelm him, that burning metal – no, behind it something else, something worse – burning *meat*. Overcooked, spoiled. The lights began to rise – too slowly, he still couldn't see anything. Except, what was that? – a faint blue light in the distance? The light in the room getting brighter now, and the Doctor could see that by his side there were drills, and there were saws, and there was an ugly electricity generator with cables running out of it towards ... what? Something at the other side of the Cage. Something which glowed blue, just a little bit, the size of a large eye.

'Hello?' he tried again, louder this time. 'Don't you worry about Van Statten, I've nothing to do with him. I'm here to help. I'm the Doctor.'

And that blue light shone more fiercely, didn't it? It *blazed*. And the Doctor heard the beginnings of a voice. Hard and rusty, like an old key trying to turn in a lock that hadn't been used for years.

Other lights now too, above the eye – because it *was* an eye, wasn't it? Raised on a stalk. Those new lights flashing in time with each hard-fought syllable that came out. As if mocking the creature's efforts to speak.

'Doc-tor,' the creature managed to say. Trying out the word to see how it felt. Trying out an old memory.

The lights in the Cage were getting brighter, and the Doctor suddenly wished they could be turned off, as if there'd be safety in the dark. Because he knew what the creature was now, and it was impossible, it was impossible.

'*The* Doctor?' The creature spoke again, and it was with greater confidence now.

It was a parody of a Dalek. Surely that's what it was. It couldn't be the real thing? The casing was shattered, cracks had been gouged into it deep and thin in a dozen places. A top section of its dome had been flattened down somehow, its blue-glowing eyestalk jutting out from it at an almost apologetic angle. Its arm was snapped like a broken twig, so that the sucker drooped uselessly and pointed towards the floor. The body was held fast with heavy chains – and those electrical cables, the Doctor could now see, ran all over the Dalek and were attached by giant clips wherever they gained purchase.

But the gunstick. The gunstick jerked into life. It pointed at the Doctor. It fired, again, and again, and again. And with it the sound of the battle cry, but with something new to it, a hysterical fury the Doctor had never heard before. 'Exterminate!' the Dalek shrieked, and it was insane, oh, it was *insane*. 'Exterminate! *Exterminate!*'

The Doctor flung himself at the door, hammered against it in panic. 'Let me out!'

And still the Dalek was screaming. 'You are an enemy of the Daleks! You must be destroyed!' And still the gun kept firing.

And still – still, the Doctor was alive.

He turned around. He laughed. He couldn't help it. He *laughed* – and there was a savagery to it that he didn't know he'd had inside him.

'Fantastic,' he said. 'Oh, fantastic. Completely powerless. Look at you. How does it *feel*?'

He ran at it, and the Dalek instinctively tried to back away; its chains groaned and held it in place. 'Keep back,' it said.

'Or what?' the Doctor shouted. He shouted right at it, right into its eyestalk. 'What are you going to do to me?'

The Dalek had no answer. The Doctor stared at it. He forced himself to speak more softly. 'If you can't kill, then what are you good for, Dalek? What's the point of you?'

Still no answer.

The Doctor realised he was shouting again, he couldn't hold it back. 'You're nothing! What the hell are you here for?'

Once again he expected no answer – but this time the Dalek spoke.

'I am waiting,' it said slowly, 'for orders.' Picking its way towards the end of the sentence as if it wasn't sure what it would find waiting there.

The statement hung in the air like a confession. Or a challenge.

'And what does that mean?'

'I am a soldier. I was bred to receive orders.'

'Well, you're never going to get any. Not ever.'

'I demand orders!' the Dalek screeched.

'And they're never going to come! Do you know why? Because your race is dead. Every single one of you, you're dead! You all burned. Ten million ships on fire. The entire Dalek fleet wiped out in one second.'

'No,' said the Dalek, and there was such anguish in its voice. 'You lie!'

'I watched it happen,' sneered the Doctor. 'I *made* it happen!'

'You destroyed the Daleks?' And the Dalek could not carry on; it choked. And for a moment the Doctor felt sorry for it. For a moment he actually wanted to offer comfort.

'I had no choice,' he said.

'And what of the Time Lords?'

'Dead. They burned with you. The end of the last Great Time War. Everybody lost.'

The Dalek spoke so softly, it was almost like a purr. 'But not you. The coward survived.'

'And what about you? Oh, I heard your little signal. "Help me." Poor little thing. Pathetic. The Dalek race would be ashamed.'

The eyestalk sagged; the Doctor thought its blue light even dimmed. He felt something like shame.

The Doctor said quietly, 'Look at me. Look at the sort of man you've turned me into.'

'I am alone,' the Dalek said. 'I am alone in the universe.'

'Yes.'

'And so are you,' said the Dalek.

The Doctor stared at it.

'We,' the Dalek said, 'are the same.'

And at that, something in the Doctor finally snapped.

He wanted to beat the Dalek, to kick it, he wanted to tear it apart with his bare hands. To put his hands through the fissures on its body, and *pull*, with all his might he'd pull them wide open, and he'd reach inside and find the little mutant cowering inside and he'd kill it. He'd kill it. And he came close – he almost touched it – he almost put himself into direct contact. And just before he did, the Doctor could sense something within the Dalek. Not fear. Not fear at all. Satisfaction? No. *Anticipation.*

The Doctor forced himself to pull back. He breathed hard.

'No,' he said. 'No, maybe you're right. Maybe you've got a point.'

He grinned. He could tell the Dalek didn't like it, that he grinned.

'You see, now I know what to do,' the Doctor went on. The rage was gone, but there was still something churning inside him, and there he was, talking away so glibly, as if trying to disguise it. 'You see, I know what comes next!' Turning away from the Dalek now, and walking to the electricity generator, almost as if he didn't have any reason to go there, almost like an afterthought. And that churning inside him, something even worse than rage, and he didn't recognise it, and it frightened him. Smiling as hard as he could. 'I know what has to happen now. I know what you *deserve*.' He took out his sonic screwdriver, and aimed it at the controls. The generator started to whine, louder and more urgently than had ever been designed.

He looked back at the Dalek. It was watching him. Of course it was watching him. 'Exterminate,' said the Doctor softly.

He pulled down hard on a lever, and at once the Dalek caught fire.

Electricity arced all around the casing and through the flames, and the acrid smell was back but so much stronger now, and the Dalek burned alive.

'Have pity!' it shrieked.

'Why should I?' the Doctor replied, and he realised that he was shrieking too. 'You never did!'

And then he felt arms around his body; the guards were in the room; they were trying to throw the lever up; there was a gun at his head. The Doctor didn't care. 'You mustn't stop me! You've got to destroy it!'

'Get him out of here!' Van Statten was shouting, and the Doctor was being dragged away from the controls, ever further away from his one chance to end the Time War again, once and for all – he was still trying to reach for them even as he was bundled out of the room.

Smoke plumed from the Dalek dome. Van Statten stood as close as he dared, but it was so *hot* – and for a terrified while he thought the Doctor had succeeded, that he had managed to murder his proudest possession. Then the Dalek turned its eyestalk upon him.

'I always knew you could talk,' said Van Statten. 'I've had such faith.'

The Dalek didn't reply.

'I saved your life! Talk to me. Goddamn it, *talk* to me!'

The eyestalk was still upon him. Was it thinking of what to say? Was it finally going to give Henry what he'd always wanted?

Van Statten licked his lips wetly. 'The last in the universe. Da-lek. Now I know your name, Da-lek. And I am Henry Van Statten. Recognise me!'

The Dalek looked away from him. It just turned the eyestalk, it looked away.

Van Statten called for Simmons. 'Make it talk again. No excuses this time. Whatever it takes.'

The Torturer's Tale

Many years later he'd be told he'd been a happy, friendly boy. The sort who was polite to grown-ups, and played well with others. And with such a lovely smile, it was a smile that could melt a room! Aaron Denton has no reason to believe that wasn't true – it's his Momma who keeps saying it, and whatever else he might think of his Momma these days, he knows Momma is no liar. And so Aaron clings on tight to that scrap of hope about his youth, he holds it in his heart. He doesn't know why. He suspects it might be important, if only for his sanity's sake.

The headaches began when he was seven. They weren't that bad at first. His parents took him to a doctor, who said they were due to eye strain. (Perhaps he needed glasses?) But the glasses didn't help. Another doctor suggested he needed more vitamin C in his diet, so he was bombarded with fresh fruit for a while. Momma was an active member of the local church, and she even got a priest to lay hands on Aaron and banish his headaches in the name of Jesus.

But nothing – not orange juice, not Jesus, not even double doses of aspirin – nothing could make the headaches stop.

He didn't get them every single day. Not at first. And then, when they *did* start coming every single day, he didn't suffer every single hour. So there was some relief to that. Often Aaron even found them tolerable; the pain was like an itch in his temples, and it was never something he could exactly *ignore*, but he could adapt to it, he could still walk and talk and think. It was silly to call it pain! And yes, it's true, sometimes the itch got so bad that he wanted to rip his head open with his fingernails, just get inside and scratch away, scratch hard until the itch was gone and his head was gone and everything, everything was gone.

But at other times, it was pain, all right. There was no pretending otherwise.

It could hit Aaron so suddenly. He'd be minding his own business – and he might even have started to hope that the doctors had been right, the headaches had just one day simply stopped all by themselves and he should have been a big boy and not made such a fuss. But then – then, in one awful instant, the pain would be back.

During an attack his body would simply freeze. If he were playing with his friends, it was as if he'd been switched off, his body would slump to the ground. If he were at the dinner table, the food would fall from his open mouth. And there was nothing except the pain, it was all the pain in the world: he'd take all his own pain and then take everyone else's pain too, just for good measure. How could so much pain be squeezed inside one poor little boy's head?

His very skull seemed to scream.

Back to the doctor's they'd go, and his parents were worried – not only for their son's sake, but for the expense, Poppa didn't have good medical insurance. A very costly X-ray of Aaron's head revealed precisely nothing. And that was good, because brain surgery would have made the price of an X-ray seem like peanuts. And it was bad news, because it meant Aaron was no closer to being cured.

But one day Aaron found the way to make the pain stop.

It had been an especially bad attack. He'd been fishing with Poppa, and Aaron hadn't caught anything but that was all right, today Poppa didn't mind, today Poppa was happy. And the pain ran him down like a freight train, and Poppa had to carry him all the way back home in his arms, and he knew Poppa would be disappointed in him once more, another day had been ruined.

Momma had the curtains in his bedroom already drawn. One of the doctors had said the darkness might help (and perhaps it even did, a bit?). And Momma put a wet flannel on his brow to cool him down. Then that was it – she'd reached the limit of her medical abilities. 'I'll pray for you, sweetie,' she said, and left him alone.

Aaron lay there in the dark, and for the first time actually wished he were dead. There was a balloon in his head, and it was slowly inflating, Aaron could feel the sticky rubber strain against his brain and against his skull and whatever else besides, and Aaron hoped that his head would just burst open, it could even make a funny little popping sound as it did so. And then – then it would all at last be over.

Through the screaming in his head he could make out other noises, *real* noises – his parents talking downstairs, too loudly, they were having another argument. A door slam. His father going out. Then, nothing – except the sound of the pain, and – yes – yes, there it was, a peculiar buzzing.

Aaron wondered what the buzzing could be. The puzzle of it was an amusing distraction. He frowned in thought, and frowning was white hot agony, but he didn't care.

He got out of bed. He rocked unsteadily on his feet. Thought he might be sick. Wasn't.

He staggered to his bedroom window. The buzzing was loudest there. Something behind the curtains.

He opened them, and the light blazed in, and his skull screamed all the louder in protest, and he told the skull to mind its own business. This was something he had to do.

On the windowsill there was a housefly. It seemed to be in some confusion. It was on its back, spinning about, unable to right itself. Drunk on the sunlight.

Aaron peered at it. It was a big, fat brute.

He wondered if the fly was happy buzzing about so noisily like that. Or perhaps it shared his pain. He hadn't the heart to shush it.

He reached out a finger. Gently placed it upon the fly's body, let it rest there. The fly seemed to thrill at his touch, quivered happily. So Aaron pressed down just a little more firmly.

Aaron knew the fly liked the comfort he was offering it.

And he pressed still harder – offering, what, more comfort? Maybe that was the idea. The fly buzzed desperately now, that was a good noise – Aaron wasn't used to noises being good. He felt its fragile body break apart under the pressure, tiny flecks of something wet smearing over his fingernail. But he didn't stop pressing, wouldn't stop pressing, wouldn't stop *crushing*, slowly now, even slower, this was something to savour. Mustn't stop – not until Aaron could feel his finger flat against the windowsill.

The fly was gone. And he was so delighted by this trick it took Aaron a full minute to realise that the headache was gone too. He stared out of the window directly into the sunlight, and it felt warm and pleasant, and it didn't hurt him at all.

Oh, it was a beautiful day.

He ran downstairs, and Momma stopped crying right away, and she was so surprised to see her brave little boy out of bed. Why, it was a miracle! She folded him in her arms and hugged him tight. And Aaron struggled out of her grasp. He told her he had things to do. And he went straight out into the garden to see if there were any more flies to be found.

He supposed at some point it became an addiction.

It wasn't that he enjoyed inflicting pain. It was a need.

'Sorry,' the little boy would whisper to the spiders he squashed, to the ants he boiled. To the daddy-long-legs as he broke off each of those long legs one by one. 'Sorry, and thank you.'

He would have liked to have stuck with insects, but as he got bigger, so the pain got bigger too. He had to move on to small animals.

He would have liked to have stuck with small animals.

At school he would target his victims carefully. He'd look out across the playground, and it was as if he had a sixth sense, he could just tell which of the other children would give his head the most relief.

There was always method to it. Sometimes he would stalk his prey for weeks before striking. The preparations were fun, and they even eased the pain a little – yes, the pain was still there, but this was good pain. It was excited pain. It was pain that egged him on.

In time he forgot to say sorry, and he forgot to say thank you.

He smiled in class. He was good at smiling, Momma always said it could melt a room. And he was unfailingly polite. He didn't want anyone to realise he was a hunter. And when he took his prey, he frightened them so much he made sure they'd never tell.

It was a *need.* It wasn't that he enjoyed inflicting pain. But we all start to enjoy the things we're good at.

Then there was that one big mistake.

Danny Simmons joined the class. And oh, he was perfect – so shy and awkward, and fat like a butterball. Danny didn't have friends, he'd just stand at the side and watch the other kids play. Aaron thought, it couldn't just be him, surely. *Everyone* must be queueing up to bully Danny Simmons.

Aaron would go to bed and dream of Danny. How juicy he was. How ripe.

Aaron got carried away, and he broke all his rules, and he forgot to be discreet.

He was expelled from school before Danny made it out of the hospital. He didn't mind being expelled. He knew it was fair. Poppa minded, though, and beat him with his belt. Aaron laughed at his Poppa. Poppa didn't know the first thing about pain. Didn't he know he couldn't hurt him – that nobody now could hurt him?

He spent the rest of his childhood being moved from school to school. Tougher schools, schools that felt like jails. His cover had been blown, and he always came to each new faculty with an ever-bulging file of psychiatric reports. And each time Aaron would charm the authorities, if only for as long as was useful – he told them he'd seen the error of his ways, he was truly penitent. He wanted to grow up and become a decent and useful member of society.

It was a great relief to everyone when he turned 16 and was old enough to leave school, go out into the real world, and offer his talents to those who could make use of them.

So, Momma comes to see him every Thursday, between the hours of three and four.

'Are they treating you well, sweetie?' she'll say. 'Are you eating enough?' He'll tell her he's fine.

And sometimes she bangs on about the old days; he wishes she wouldn't. 'You were such a happy boy. So friendly. Do you remember? Oh, tell me you remember! And you had such a lovely smile! A smile that could melt a room!'

She'll be crying by this point, and that's just embarrassing. Aaron tries to cheer her up with a smile, but he's not good at smiling any more, he's lost the knack. Now when he smiles he shows far too many teeth. 'It'll all be better when you get out,' she promises him. 'You can live with me, and we'll find you a nice job. It's not too late for us.'

His toothy smile widens until he thinks his face will split, and he thinks *shut up shut up shut up*. He thinks, *I'm never getting out of here, don't you understand?*

But he won't tell her because Aaron doesn't want to hurt his Momma.

After her weekly visit, Aaron usually goes to work in the laundry. His head will be pounding, and he finds he can relieve it a little by steaming beds and trousers and bed linen, he can imagine he's steaming to death every single person in the prison.

One Thursday when he goes to laundry, a guard stops him. 'You've got a visitor,' he's told.

'I've already seen her,' says Aaron. He has no desire to see her again.

'It's not a her,' says the guard. 'And your visitor doesn't want to be kept waiting.'

Aaron is taken to a room he's never seen before. Thick carpet, tables and chairs that aren't made out of plastic. No glass partition to speak through. A dainty man with a neat beard and fierce little eyes sits on one of those chairs that look so wonderfully soft, and half rises in acknowledgement as Aaron comes in. 'Mr Denton,' the man says. 'Please, join me.'

And then, most astonishing of all, the man simply nods curtly at the guard, and the guard leaves them alone.

'What is this?' growls Aaron. He wants to hit this man. He knows how good that would feel. He knows how delicious, to rip his smug head off his smug suited body.

The man smiles benignly, as if Aaron is an old friend who's just made a polite enquiry about his health. 'Tell me, Mr Denton,' he says, 'how would you like another life than this?'

And he breaks into a big, hearty laugh – and Aaron laughs too, he can't help it.

'Sure,' says Aaron. 'Why not? That would be nice.'

'I can do it. One word from me, and you can be out of here this evening, all charges dropped. I have a certain influence.' The man stops laughing, and Aaron knows he's speaking the truth.

'Who are you?'

'That's the wrong question.'

'What do you want me to do?'

'Better,' says the man. 'I have a friend I care for very deeply. And for some reason, no matter how much I ask him, he won't talk to me.'

Aaron says, 'I can make anyone talk.'

'You can have a new identity. A whole new life. Everything you have ever done, every past mistake, all wiped away. It's a fresh start, Mr Denton. Or Mr whatever name you like.'

The man takes out a piece of paper that is pure white, and crisp, and soft. He slides it across the table. Aaron picks it up, looks at it. Written on it is a nearby address.

'Be there tomorrow morning at eight o'clock sharp, and a helicopter will take you very far from here, and you will never want for anything ever again.'

'And,' says Aaron, 'what's to stop me simply disappearing, and you never see me again?'

The man chuckles. 'What a funny idea!' he says. 'You can even try, if you like!'

Aaron knows he won't run. He doesn't like this man. He has been employed by a lot of bad men over the years, and he knows how to read them. But this is a man he cannot read, and that frightens him. And what frightens him the most is that he can't work out precisely how frightened he should be.

But one thing is clear. His headache has gone. For the first time since he's been put in prison, just by sitting with this man for five minutes. The pain has melted away to nothing.

'You'll give me a new identity?' Aaron asks. 'Everything I've ever done wiped away?'

'Yes.'

'Up until eight o'clock tomorrow morning? Everything I have ever done, up until then?'

The man smiles thinly. 'If you wish.'

Aaron Denton offers his hand. The man says, 'That won't be necessary.'

And the man makes to leave, and Aaron knows that he has to ask one last question. Even if it ruins everything, even if it costs him this brand new future he now so eagerly wants. 'Stop,' he says – and the man stops; he turns around, he fixes Aaron with those fierce little eyes, he shows he is not accustomed to stopping for anyone.

'Why me?' says Aaron, and his voice is soft, it makes him sound like a little boy. Someone who is polite to grown-ups and plays well with others.

'I am Henry Van Statten,' replies the man. 'And I only take the best.'

He doesn't leave the room immediately, some instinct tells him he doesn't want to follow too close on Henry Van Statten's heels. He waits a few minutes. And then at last he leaves the room too, and he knows this isn't a joke, he knows this is desperately and dangerously real, and that his life has subtly changed forever – but what if it *is* a joke, what if the guards outside are waiting for him, what if they laugh?

There are no guards outside, nor in the corridors, nor by the open door leading to freedom. It is as if they are all hiding from him.

It occurs to Aaron that he will never see his Momma again, and she will never find out what has happened to him. His stomach clenches, just for a second, and then he puts the thought away for good.

Outside the prison Aaron Denton finds waiting for him a brand new car. There is a suitcase full of clothes, an envelope full of money, and keys dangling in the ignition.

*

Aaron Denton has chosen his new name, but he isn't ready to own it yet. He practises the sound of it in his mouth. He likes the way it rolled off his tongue. He can hardly wait for it to be his.

He has already driven well over an hour, back to the town where he had grown up. And now he's forced to wait, staring at the front door of a pretty little house on a pretty residential street in the suburbs. It has always been peaceful, Aaron knows, nothing bad ever happens here. People smile as they pass each other on the sidewalk – they even smile at the strange man sitting in his car and speaking his new name over and over again. No one seems to find him suspicious.

Once upon a time Aaron loved to wait. It was all part of the fun of stalking his prey. Perhaps he's out of the habit now, because he begins to get worried. He's thinking of the address Van Statten gave him, and how he mustn't be late for the rendezvous – it makes him start to fidget, his hands itch. Another itch growing, his head beginning to smart. The hours pass. The sidewalk empties; it's dusk now; it's dark. It would be safer to abort the mission. It would be safer to leave right now. Do not be late for the rendezvous, he doesn't want to think what they might do to him. But he doesn't want to leave, he *won't* leave, this is all he wants, these last few precious hours as Aaron Denton, and he is going to use them well. (But what if all this waiting is for nothing?) It is not for nothing. (But what if the man has moved away?) He has not moved away. All these years, he's made sure to keep up to date. Be patient. He was once so good at patience! Be patient, and ignore the itches.

And there – oh, praise Jesus – there, at last, he sees him. A little man crossing the road, and walking up the path to his home. Still fat like a butterball. Hobbling slowly on his one good leg.

There is no need to rush now. Aaron yearns for him, but he can afford to enjoy the anticipation. Let the poor man relax for a while, make himself comfortable first. It is the least he can do for him.

But Aaron has waited such a long time already, and he can only be so generous. At last he gets out of the car. He fetches his toolkit from the trunk.

When Danny Simmons opens the door, Aaron can see he's been recognised, and that makes him happy. It's touching to know that after all these years he's mattered to Danny just as Danny has mattered to him. 'I'm sorry,' says Aaron kindly, even tenderly, and it's nice to say sorry to his prey once more, just as he'd do when he was a little kid. 'I'm sorry, but we have unfinished business.'

He steps inside the house, and closes the door.

4

'Oh, I have such plans for you, Doctor,' said Van Statten.

The Doctor was tied to a chair. He glared, and said nothing.

'On the one hand,' Van Statten went on, 'you tried to destroy the centrepiece of my collection. An utterly priceless artefact, the only one in existence. I should be very angry. On the other hand …'

'Yeah, tell me what's on the other hand.'

'On the other hand, you did get it to talk. It's almost lively now! I like it lively. Perhaps the two hands cancel each other out. Perhaps I can even be grateful. What do you think?'

The Doctor strained against his ropes. 'Yeah, your gratitude is overwhelming. If you want to be grateful, then just listen to me. Let me explain to you what a Dalek is.'

So the Doctor told him how the Daleks had evolved as mutants emerging from an atomic war, now genetically engineered to fight for the survival of their race. Told him that all emotions had been erased from them, or warped into hatred, a psychopathic loathing of all other species. That they had spread through the universe like a plague, subjugating countless civilisations, and destroying where they couldn't subjugate. That their immediate impulse was always to kill.

And Van Statten sat down with the Doctor and listened. He even believed.

'All right, Doctor,' he said at last. 'But what harm, really, can it do? You've already demonstrated, its weaponry doesn't even work.'

'It doesn't need weapons,' said the Doctor. 'It's ruthless, and more intelligent than anything on your planet. It has a genius you couldn't even begin to understand. Even talking to it is dangerous. You mustn't let it get inside your head.'

'But that's the whole point,' Van Statten argued. 'It *doesn't* talk. And it's been on Earth for over 50 years, moving around from private collection to private collection. And look what's happened! Nothing. No Armageddon. The end of the world hasn't taken place. We're all still alive. Why would it become a threat now?'

'Isn't it obvious? Because I'm here. *Because I'm here.*'

Van Statten thought about this for a while.

The Doctor went on, 'It must have fallen through time. The only survivor in a war between my people and its people. It'll want to finish the job.'

‘As do you, Doctor. You want to finish the job. Win your war.’

The Doctor looked away from Van Statten sullenly. ‘It isn’t like that.’

Van Statten got to his feet, and the Doctor realised that the interview was over, and he had failed.

‘You talk of genius,’ Van Statten said. ‘But I can’t help but notice: I’ve got the Dalek. I’ve got you. Maybe you underestimate *my* genius.’

The Doctor laughed coldly. ‘Your genius? Look around you. All you do is feed off other people’s skills. You’re a thief.’

Van Statten looked so angry the Doctor thought he was going to hit him. But Van Statten refused; he smoothed his beard hard, as if it were the source of all his temper, and by flattening it into submission he could keep himself under control. Then he said, ‘Maybe you’re right. Maybe I am a thief. All my great achievements, I’ve made them climbing upon the shoulders of others. But to succeed, you have to know exactly whose shoulders to climb. And you must admit, for that I have a certain genius. I only steal from the very best. And what about you, Doctor? Aren’t you the best? I rather think that you are.’

He gave a signal, and guards hauled the Doctor to his feet. They had been in the shadows, and the Doctor hadn’t even realised they were there.

'The Dalek is no longer the only living alien in my museum, Doctor. Now I have you too. The last of your kind.'

So they dragged the Doctor to a laboratory. They stripped him, and hung him up by manacles. Van Statten expressed some disappointment that his new alien looked so very human and ordinary, but he was delighted when the laser scan pierced the Doctor's chest and revealed two hearts and a binary vascular system.

'I am so going to patent this,' Van Statten said.

'Quite a step!' the Doctor spat through the pain. 'From world wide web to alien vivisection.'

'My alien collection is the foundation for my entire empire. It's made me billions. Broadband; the cure for cancer? Both discovered in the same meteorite, in this very room. Broadband's been a great success. And the cancer cure? I'm just waiting until the accountants tell me it's financially viable.'

'Picking through the rubbish bins of civilisations greater than your own. You must be very proud.'

'Oh, I am.'

'One more thing about a Dalek,' the Doctor gasped, as another laser beam swept over his body. 'A Dalek is pure. It does what it was born to do for the greater good of its kind. That creature in your dungeon is better than you.'

'What sort of alien are you, Doctor? Tell me about your people. I want to know everything.'

'My people are irrelevant!' the Doctor shouted. 'They're all dead, and so will you be! The Dalek knows I'm here, and when it gets out, it won't stop until it's killed every last one of us!'

He didn't know whether Van Statten had any answer to that. Because that was the point when the laser beam reached his head, and the Doctor blacked out.

The English kid's workshop was a mess, bits of rock and metal strewn over the desk and the floor in random order. 'Sorry,' he said gruffly. 'Didn't realise I'd have to share the room. Clear a space, wherever you like.'

Rose was used to boys being nervous around her. She remembered only too well that summer holiday when she was 13, and her mum said she had 'blossomed' – all she'd known was that when she went back to school in September half of the class started acting weirdly around her. Friends she'd known for years suddenly being shy, or ignoring her altogether. But this boy was different. He wasn't stealing glances at her when he hoped she wasn't looking. He wasn't trying to impress her.

He was even reluctant to tell her his name. As if it would give too much away, as if it would make him vulnerable somehow. 'Adam Mitchell,' he said to her at last.

'Don't you mind your boss not knowing that?' she asked.

No,' he said bluntly. And then added, 'It's a relief.'

Rose decided to change the subject. She picked up something she supposed looked vaguely alien off the floor; it crumbled to dust in her hand, and she hoped Adam hadn't noticed. 'What is all this stuff?'

'These are alien artefacts of incalculable wealth and power.'

'Really?'

'Or they will be, when I've finished with them. Here,' Adam said, and tossed her something the size and shape of a pebble, 'what do you make of that?'

She stared down at it. 'I don't know. A lump of metal?'

Adam said, 'Well, I think ... I'm almost certain, actually ... that it's from the hull of a spacecraft. I've found others like it, they all slot together, they're strange. It keeps happening, you put them together, all these things that look like nothing, and they start to have meaning. I mean, it all seems like junk at first, but if you can just find the right context, they're fantastic. Absolutely fantastic.' He grinned at her suddenly, and his eyes sparkled with real excitement, and Rose thought, he's just like the Doctor. Or could be. If he were given half a chance.

And then the moment was gone. Adam seemed to remember himself, that he didn't trust Rose, that he didn't trust himself. He became the awkward English kid once more, and looked down at his desk.

'Why do you do this?' asked Rose. 'Why do you want to live like this?'

Adam still didn't look up. 'I was recruited. Mr Van Statten has agents all around the world looking for geniuses.'

'Ah,' said Rose. 'So, you're a genius.'

Adam said softly, 'It felt good to be wanted.' And he looked up, and at her properly for the first time, and Rose could see he wasn't sulking, and he wasn't shy – Adam was scared. 'I'm in charge of the inanimates,' he said. 'Anything alien that hasn't got a pulse, that's my job. And Mr Van Statten wants to give that job to you.'

Rose laughed. 'I'm not having your job! He was joking!'

'Mr Van Statten makes lots of jokes,' said Adam. 'The thing is, most of them end up coming true.'

'Well, I'm not interested,' said Rose. 'I'm not spending my life underground. I'd rather spend my life out there. Among the stars. Wouldn't you?'

Adam stared at her. 'I'd give anything,' he said. 'Absolutely anything.'

Rose smiled. He smiled back, a little nervously.

'But it'll never happen in our lifetimes,' he said, and looked away.

'Yeah,' said Rose. 'You're probably right. But still, I shan't waste my life surrounded by lumps of metal. Even if they are from spaceship hulls. I think I'd rather take my chances with something that's alive. There's a real alien creature downstairs.'

'I went to see it,' said Adam. 'Just the once.'

'And?'

Adam shook his head, as if to chase away a bad memory. 'And nothing. It isn't very interesting. Like a great useless pepperpot, just sits there and doesn't do anything.'

'Can you show me?'

'It's off limits,' said Adam. 'But there's a live video feed, I sometimes hack in and take a look.'

'Well, let's see then.'

Adam worked at his computer, then let Rose see the screen. The image was blurred, and the room was dark. She squinted at the creature. And just briefly she was disappointed – Adam was right, it wasn't very impressive. She could vaguely make out a shape, it was just another lump of metal, wasn't it? Just a bigger lump of metal than the lumps scattered around Adam's workshop.

Then she saw a man in protective clothing enter the frame. He was carrying a drill.

Soon the lump of metal started to scream. The same scream she had heard in the TARDIS.

'They're torturing it,' she said. She whirled around to Adam, and saw with relief that he was shocked too, he had nothing to do with this. 'We've got to tell the Doctor. Where is he?'

'I don't know.'

'Then take me down there. Now.'

Adam Mitchell knew that, on paper at least, he and Danny Simmons had the same job. They were both responsible for the cataloguing of alien artefacts. Adam didn't always understand people very well – they were so very complex with their unreadable body languages – but he knew Simmons and he had nothing in common, and that his method of caring for the collection was very different from his own. He had only met him the once, and that encounter had terrified him, and ever since he had been grateful there were over fifty floors of thick concrete keeping the two of them apart.

He had no idea how he could persuade Simmons to give Rose access to the creature in the Cage. And, like most very clever people, had Adam been given the time to work out a plan, he would have thought about it too hard and made the plan too elaborate, and he would have ruined everything. But there *wasn't* the time – Rose was angry and insistent, she was going to help the tortured animal, no matter what.

'She wants to see it,' said Adam bluntly.

'All right,' said Simmons, just as bluntly back. He was sweating inside his protective uniform. He'd just been engaged in an especially physical attempt to persuade the Dalek to speak again, and it hadn't gone well. 'The Doctor got it to talk. Maybe his friend can get a few words out of it too. She can go in.'

Rose didn't bother to respond; she strode inside the Cage.

Simmons gave Adam a smile, one of his toothiest. 'On condition that you go in with her.'

Rose could see the creature clearly at last, and she recoiled. Now it seemed impossibly, appallingly alien. Even with all the other species she had met on her travels, Rose had a sudden and almost primal sense that this was the most alien thing she had ever seen. It was wrong. Everything about it told her it was wrong. She wanted to run. She wanted to get as far away from it as possible.

Instead, she made herself walk all the way up to it. Close.

Rose remembered when the Doctor had taken her to Platform One. Her first trip off planet – and he'd dropped her in the middle of a party teeming with extraterrestrials, and she'd been revolted. She wasn't able to stop herself – it had been overwhelming, too much for her brain to take in.

And the Doctor had been disappointed in her. He'd thought she was better than that. And she'd wanted to be better. 'Imagine what you must look like to them,' he'd said. So that's what she tried to do now. How would she feel if *she* were the metal pepperpot, and she was the one imprisoned, and surrounded by fleshy creatures with arms and legs sticking out, with faces that opened up to show their insides whenever they tried to communicate? Wouldn't that pepperpot be revolted too? Wouldn't it be terrified?

'Don't get too close,' she heard Adam say. She ignored him.

'Hello,' said Rose, very softly. 'Can you hear me?'

The creature didn't move. What if it couldn't hear her? What if it didn't even have ears? Or if she were simply whispering into its elbow?

'Are you in pain?' she went on. 'My name's Rose Tyler. What's your name?' She felt absurd, introducing herself like that.

A memory – a man called Clive had once shown her information he had spent years collecting about the Doctor. There were so many pictures of aliens, and they had all looked rather ridiculous, like men in rubber suits – she had barely paid attention. Hadn't this pepperpot been one of them?

'I've got a friend who can help you. Maybe you know him? He's called the Doctor.'

And at that the eyestalk swung into life with surprising speed, and at last looked at her.

'Yes,' said the creature.

'What?'

'Yes,' it said again, and the voice was low, and grating, and seemed so old and so sad. 'I am in pain. They torture me. And yet still they fear me. Do you fear me, Rose Tyler?'

'No,' Rose lied. And yet, it wasn't entirely a lie, was it? Not really.

'Come closer,' it said.

She did.

'I am dying,' said the creature. It didn't sound sorry for itself. It came out as a statement of fact. Perhaps that's what tore at Rose's heart the most.

'We can help,' she said, though she didn't know if they could.

'I welcome death. But I am glad. That before I died. I have met a human who was not afraid.'

'There must be something I can do.'

'Come closer still.'

And still, she did.

'My race is dead. I am the last of my kind. Touch me. So I shall not die alone.'

And that was when Rose stretched out her hand and placed it upon the Dalek dome.

'No!' shouted Adam. 'Don't!'

But it was too late.

The Doctor awoke to the lights in the laboratory flashing on and off as the electricity surged and fell; he heard Goddard's panic as she shouted over the intercom that this was an emergency, condition red, *condition red* – and Van Statten was shaking him, and at long last the little man looked afraid.

'Release me,' said the Doctor, 'if you want to live.'

*

The Dalek was screaming once more, not in pain this time, but in triumph. 'Genetic material extrapolated!' it exulted. 'Am initiating cellular reconstruction!'

Rose backed away in horrified wonder as the creature rebuilt itself. The eerie golden glow that surrounded it was dazzling – it seemed to be offering new life, and new hope, but what else besides? And through it she could see the dents of the casing smooth away, the deep gashes cut into the sides fusing back together. The chains that had held the creature down were snapping one by one like thread.

She felt an arm pull at her, and she began to fight it off – but it was Adam. Dragging her towards the door. Towards safety.

'What the hell have you done?' shouted Simmons. He ran to the Dalek, trusty drill in hand.

He stared as even the Dalek's snapped arm healed itself, the broken stick reforming, becoming strong. Its silly little sink plunger pointed straight up at him.

'And what are you going to do with that?' he sneered. 'Sucker me to death?'

It was as if the Dalek decided to take his suggestion. The arm extended, and the sucker was on his face now, closing hard over his mouth. Then he could feel the sucker *squeeze*, and he'd always supposed it was made out of rubber, but it really was nothing remotely like rubber at all.

And the headache was back. Little Aaron Denton's headache was reporting in, present and correct. *Did you miss me?* it screamed at him. *Did you think I'd ever really gone away?* And he supposed he had missed the headaches somehow. They had defined him. He almost welcomed the pain as an old friend.

Aaron felt the sucker was on the move, wriggling further across his face. It had tiny fingers, they were grabbing for purchase and then pulling the sucker up, now over his nose, over his eyes. A burning oil slick pouring up his nostrils and into his tear ducts. And *squeezing*. The headache got louder and wider than he had ever known it, the pain was his entire world. And Aaron didn't know whether to laugh or to scream, and he didn't do either, because he wasn't *able* to do either, the Dalek sucker had pooled over his entire face by now, he couldn't see, he couldn't breathe. Still squeezing, ever tighter, it was an ecstasy of agony, there was no end to it – and then there was – at last there was – because Aaron heard something crack, and he idly wondered whether it was his skull. And at last the headache was cured.

The Collector's Tale

On his seventh birthday, Henry received a present from his father. He was delighted – and surprised too, because he hadn't received one on his sixth.

Of course, he didn't get it from his father directly. Edward Van Statten was on a business trip in Eastern Europe, and Henry hadn't seen him in months. Instead the present was brought to him by Otto, one of his father's personal assistants.

'What's inside, do you think?' Otto asked. The present was hidden beneath shiny wrapping paper, and his father would have found that frivolous, so Henry knew Otto must have wrapped it himself. But Otto continued to act excited on Henry's behalf.

'It's a telescope!' said Henry.

'So it is. Shall we set it up?'

Henry's father had several houses all over the world, but the most remote was the one he kept his son in, built in the Utah desert. Edward Van Statten called the Utah base his centre of operations – wholly isolated, away from the spying eyes of competition. There were no other buildings for 50 miles in any direction – Van Statten made sure of that – so while there were no business rivals, there was also no one for a young boy to play with. Henry had never been allowed to visit any of his father's other houses, not in Rome or Moscow, not in London or Tokyo. He hoped he might some day.

'You wouldn't want to be at any of them,' Otto had told Henry once. 'In the middle of a city, where there's so much noise! And when at night you look up into the sky, the light pollution means you can't make out the stars. This is the best place, Henry. A man should always be able to see the stars above his head.'

The telescope was so large that Otto had to carry it up to Henry's bedroom for him. He spent an hour assembling it, while Henry sat on his bed and waited. Henry wasn't sure whether he should be excited or bored. Otto worked hard, and when Henry saw just how much care he was devoting to the task, he decided to be excited.

'Thank you, Otto,' said Henry, and he gave him a hug. And then wished he hadn't, because Otto always got stiff and formal when he did something like that.

'You can work out the rest for yourself,' said Otto gruffly. 'Good night, then, and happy birthday.'

Henry looked through the telescope. He worked out how to point it, how to adjust the focus. There were thousands of stars to look at. Some were grouped together in tight bunches. Some, it seemed, were all alone in the pitch-black sky. Alone and adrift, like him.

It was pretty, but after a little while Henry's attention began to wane. It was pointless just staring up into space if he didn't know what he was looking at. He needed information. He needed facts. And he was about to give up on the telescope for good and go to bed when he heard a faint knock at his door. When he opened it, there was no one there. But lying on the floor was a big book about astronomy.

Henry stayed up all night, and then all day, and the next night too. Gazing into infinity, then studying what he'd seen in the book. He tried to map the whole universe.

The next time Henry saw Otto he was able to show him Mars, Venus and Jupiter. The time after, Henry was pointing out all the constellations.

'But why do you think my father bought me a telescope?' he asked.

Otto said, 'It's an object lesson, Henry. Your father wants you to realise the world is vast and full of opportunities. And your ambitions should be as far-reaching as the stars.'

'I see,' said Henry, dubiously.

They both fiddled with the telescope for a while, in companionable silence.

'Tell me,' Henry said. 'Do you think there could be life on other planets?'

Otto thought about this long and hard, and then said, gravely, 'No, Henry, I don't.'

'You're wrong.'

One day Henry's father came home. Henry only knew this because there was such a sudden flurry of activity at the base, everybody running about trying to impress. And a few mornings later Henry received a written instruction to join his father for breakfast.

Father and son sat in the dining room together, and ate bacon and eggs with silver cutlery. 'Our Russian merger has been most successful,' Henry was told, 'and one day you'll have the necessary acumen to be grateful. And what about you? Have you been studying hard?'

'Yes, Father.'

'Which economic theories have you been exploring?'

'The Keynesian and the Friedmanite models.'

'Excellent.'

'And I have also been studying the stars. Thank you, Father, for my telescope. It is the best present I have ever had.'

Edward Van Statten never bothered to raise his voice in anger, and he certainly wasn't going to do so now. He dabbed a dribble of egg yolk away from his mouth with a serviette, and told the waiter to fetch Otto von Dönitz immediately.

As soon as Otto entered the room, Henry could tell something was very wrong. Otto, hulking like a bodyguard, already seemed hunched and cowed. 'Mr Van Statten, sir,' he began.

Father interrupted him. 'You were told to buy my son something purposeful and instructive.'

'Yes, sir.'

'You bought him a telescope.'

'I did, sir.'

'Thank you, von Dönitz. You may go.'

Otto turned to Henry, and there was something almost pleading in that look. Henry didn't know what he wanted from him. He looked down hard at the breakfast table.

'You may go,' Van Statten insisted.

Otto left.

'Father,' Henry began, 'it shows me the world is vast and full of opportunities.'

'No. It shows us there are places we can never reach, and goals we can never achieve. It is defeatism writ large. I shall not have defeatism in my house. You shall take this telescope, and you shall destroy it. I want you to break it apart, piece by piece, and bring those pieces to me. And then we shall dispose of them together.'

It was another six weeks before Henry saw his father again, and when he met him the next time over breakfast the matter wasn't mentioned. Henry began to hope that the telescope may have been forgotten; he even dared one night to pull it out from under his bed, take it to the window, and gaze out at the stars once more. But one day, nearing Christmas, Van Statten said to Henry, 'I think I have been patient long enough, don't you?' And Henry brought down the telescope, and watched as Father's henchmen hurled it to the ground and stamped upon it. Edward Van Statten didn't force Henry to break it himself – he wasn't entirely without compassion.

Henry never saw Otto again. For a while he wondered where he might be, whether he was happy. And then he forgot all about him.

And on his 15th birthday, his father gave Henry a million dollars.

'It's not a present,' Edward said when Henry tried to thank him. 'Frankly, I'd completely forgotten it was your birthday, that's a complete coincidence. No, this is a test.'

So Henry asked what this test entailed.

'Here's the situation,' said Edward. 'I'm dying. The heart, probably, they say I shan't see out the year. And I want to safeguard the future of Van Statten Corporation, I'm going to protect my legacy. As my only son you are my natural successor, but I want to make sure you're worthy.'

Henry expressed some regret for his father's impending demise, and asked exactly what he could do to ascertain that worthiness.

'I'll give you three months,' his father said. 'Take the million, and invest it wisely. Let me see what sort of profit you can make.'

Henry thanked him for the opportunity, but Edward told him to be silent.

'Listen. This is a dictatorship, not a monarchy,' he said. 'The son does not automatically inherit the crown, you understand? Let me down, and I'll happily turn over all my assets to the lawyers, they can carve up my empire for themselves, and I'll leave you penniless. All right?'

To help him pass the test, Edward Van Statten assigned a crack team of financial advisers to Henry's side. The very same day Henry informed them that their assistance would not be required.

Precisely three months later Henry was recalled to see his father. The financial advisers were there too, standing around his father's desk in a ring, each looking rather sullen and resentful.

'The million dollars,' Henry's father said. 'What profit have you made?'

'None,' replied Henry.

'And how much have you spent?'

'All of it,' said Henry. 'Every last cent.'

'Are you a fool?'

'That remains to be seen.' And Henry smiled. He had never dared smile in front of his father before.

Edward Van Statten, rarely, didn't know what to say. At last one of the advisory team knelt beside him and whispered in his ear.

‘Van Statten Corporation has established itself through the trade of oils and arms,’ said Edward. ‘I am told you have chosen to invest elsewhere.’

‘I have put our money,’ said Henry, ‘into global communications. It is the future. Oil is too obvious, and arms is too crude. If the Van Statten name is to survive, it needs to have more vision than you have ever shown, Father, and be bolder than you have ever had the stomach for.’

Once again, an adviser dropped down beside Edward Van Statten to hiss something at him. This time, Edward swatted him away like a fly. ‘In three months there has been no financial return.’

‘Do you know how long it takes a rocket to reach Jupiter? Six years. It travels 365 million miles through nothing but empty space. Cancel the operation five years in, you get nothing. But in the sixth year, if you’re patient, finally, you win a new world.’

‘Are you suggesting we won’t see my return back for six whole years?’

‘Six years, sixteen years, *sixty*!’ Henry laughed. ‘Jupiter is nothing! Who cares about Jupiter? I intend to go much farther. So, Father, now *you* listen, *you* understand. The company as you know it is dead. The world is changing, and you’re too old to see it. Cut me off without a dime, I don’t care. I shall find my way. Or trust me, and your legacy will be secure.’

One final time the financial advisers tried to talk, and at last he lost his temper – Edward Van Statten, who with all his power had never needed to raise his voice, now raged for the first time in 50 years. 'Get out!' he shouted. 'Get out, all of you! You are dismissed!'

Father and son were left on their own.

'I'm not really dying,' Edward said to his son. 'That was just part of the test.'

'I don't care,' said Henry Van Statten. 'Cede your business to me today. It is my time to shine.'

And that is exactly what his father did.

Edward Van Statten did die eventually, but by that time his life no longer really mattered. Long before, Van Statten Corporation had been renamed Geocomtex, and Henry ignored his father's feeble protests. 'I prefer the subtlety of anonymity,' he had told him. On the day of the funeral Henry paid him full respect, and instructed everyone in the corporation to set aside work for ten whole minutes of silent mourning.

To pursue his dream of communications supremacy, Henry Van Statten sent agents all over the world to recruit men of particular genius. Together they put the internet into every home in the developed world. It was global domination of a sort; Henry thought his father might even have been proud. He threw a party for all the scientific teams who had helped him; they all stood around and ate canapés and drank champagne. The leader said, 'None of us ever really believed the internet would be so successful!'

'None of you believed it?' asked Henry. 'Well, well.' And he had them all fired.

But it wasn't enough. It was never enough. And sometimes he would return to his offices in Rome and in Moscow, in London and in Tokyo, and there he'd idly play with the telescope he kept upon his desk in every one. He'd stare out at the night sky.

At first even Van Statten thought that the decision to collect artefacts from space was just a rich man's hobby. He bought moon rocks, asteroid boulders, tiny pebbles mined from Mars. He put them on his desks alongside the telescopes. He used them as paperweights.

It was after the dissolution of his second marriage that Henry decided he should commit to his hobby properly.

There are secrets shared by the great billionaires, stories of extraterrestrial objects far more spectacular than mere planetary debris. The billionaires didn't want Van Statten to be part of their club; they didn't like him; he didn't belong. But it's hard to keep secrets from a man who owns the internet.

Most sold their collections to him fairly simply. Those who were drawn to the alien because it was exotic and expensive were easy targets – there are always things still more exotic and expensive one can offer in return. They hadn't always treated their treasures with respect. Van Statten was scandalised. Milo Rothenberg had used the fuel gauge for the Roswell spacecraft as an ashtray. The Sabatini family let their children each year use the Slitheen arm as part of a Halloween costume.

Some collectors required more persuasion, but Van Statten eventually got what he wanted.

And soon he had acquired so much alien exotica he could dream of owning a museum. A private museum, of course, just for him. He knew no one else could possibly appreciate it.

Henry did what he vowed as a child he would never do. He went back to Utah. Not to his father's base, of course – he'd had that razed to the ground, he wanted no part of that. Instead, in its ruins, he would build *downward*. His base would be underground, somewhere he could keep his collection secure. Architects designed him a vast complex ten storeys deep – it wasn't enough. They doubled it – twenty storeys – still not enough. 'But how deep do you want us to go?' they begged him. Van Statten laughed, and pointed at the sky, so vast, so infinite, and told them there should be no end to it.

And once more his agents scoured the world for experts, but now the genius he sought was in the extraterrestrial. Astronomists, theorists, even science fiction writers – anyone with an imagination to see beyond the earthbound and the humdrum was required. And scientists working half a mile beneath the surface would discover unexpected benefits to Van

Statten's growing mania. Broadband and Bluetooth, side effects of spaceship crashes. There were cures for famine, and cures for plague; there were three separate cures discovered for the common cold.

Sometimes Henry Van Statten would even pretend there was a genuine altruistic point to his collection. That, secretly, he laboured only to serve mankind. As he locked the latest medical breakthroughs up tight in a safe, waiting to see whether they would ever become marketable.

On his 45th birthday, Henry Van Statten decided to get himself a present.

There had long been rumours of living alien matter housed in private collections. And Van Statten would pay over the odds to get it, and yet was always disappointed – the microbes inside the Martian rocks he'd been promised were either dead or had long since vacated the premises. He had resigned himself to the idea that however large his museum may grow, it would really only be a *museum*, a collection of the past.

But there was growing interest in an old rumour. An alien creature that had fallen to Earth some 40 years ago. It had caused an impact crater some hundred feet deep in the Ascension Islands, and it had cost the lives of three men to get it out. And it was alive. Screaming as it burned, but alive.

The rumour had persisted for years, and Van Statten had never dared believe it. But it had broken cover.

Hidden away discreetly since its arrival, the alien had finally been sold in private auction – but not so private that his agents hadn't heard about it.

It was larger than a man. No more stupid dead microbes. This was something truly tangible. Van Statten had to have it.

His spies confirmed that it was in the possession of one Hiram Duchesne. Van Statten had never heard of him. Why, the man only had a couple of million to his name, and that was all tied up in some frozen dessert company. He didn't deserve to own such a trophy.

When on his birthday Van Statten flew out to see Duchesne, he didn't expect any great difficulty. 'I want to buy your creature,' he said. 'I shall give you five million dollars.'

'No sale,' said Duchesne, and walked out of the conference room, and no matter how long Van Statten waited, he would not be summoned back.

Van Statten didn't give up. He sent out further offers. He didn't mind being generous. He would pay seven million dollars. 'No.' Ten million. 'Over my dead body.' Twenty-five million dollars, what about twenty-five? Duchesne didn't even deign to reply.

So Van Statten decided to persuade Duchesne by other means. He called a meeting of the Geocomtex board. 'For years our direction has been in global communications,' he told them. 'It's time to diversify. Let's seize control of the ice cream market.'

Duchesne's company was pushed to the brink of bankruptcy. 'How does that 25 million look now?' Van Statten messaged him. It did no good.

And then, one day, Van Statten received a formal letter from Hiram Duchesne, politely requesting his attention for a proposal he sought to make. Van Statten ordered his private helicopter into action immediately.

Hiram Duchesne was too weak to take a meeting in his conference room; instead he lay in bed, and he was so *thin*, and pale, and his face was sweating. 'You still want my monster?' he croaked.

'Of course,' said Van Statten.

'I'll take your 25 million, on one condition. They say that in your labs, experimenting on alien tissue, that you've found,' Duchesne licked cracked lips, 'the cure for cancer.'

Van Statten said nothing.

'You can take my monster. Twenty-five million, and the cure.'

Still, Van Statten said nothing, but he started to smile.

'All right! All right. Forget the money. You can keep your money. Just give me the cure. Please! Save my life.' And Duchesne was so excited he coughed for a full minute, and Van Statten waited for him to stop before speaking.

'How advanced is it?' he asked gently.

'It's pretty bad,' said Duchesne, and gave a brave smile.

'You know,' said Van Statten, and he took hold of the sick man's hand, and it was transparent like tracing paper, Van Statten thought it could so easily just *snap* – 'You know, I've been very patient. I suppose I can be patient a little longer, and just wait until you're dead.'

And for just a moment Duchesne stared at him in horror; he tried to pull his hand away, but Van Statten wouldn't let him.

Then Duchesne smiled, and it was a thin bitter smile, and Van Statten was surprised by the dying man's strength as he pulled him close.

'Very well,' rasped the man in Van Statten's ear. 'You'll get my monster. I hope you enjoy him, Van Statten. But listen to him very carefully. Listen to everything he has to say.'

'It can talk?'

'Oh yes!' Duchesne's skeletal face broke out into a broken grin. 'Oh, all the wonders he has to share!'

Van Statten flew back to Utah, and waited for his monster to be sent to him. It didn't take long. A large wooden crate was set down upon the desert floor, and Van Statten pressed his ear against the side. He could hear nothing. There was no reason to think there was anything alive in there, let alone anything alien. But Van Statten *believed*. He *knew*.

'My 45th birthday present,' he said. By this time Henry Van Statten was 53.

*

The moment Dr Yevgeny Kandinsky got in from Ukraine, Goddard took him down to the lower vaults. He complained that he was tired and hungry, but Van Statten didn't care – he was eager to see the cosmologist's first impressions of the creature. He was disappointed. Kandinsky stared at it. Then he took off his glasses, absently rubbed at the lens. 'Interesting,' he said, finally.

'Only interesting?' said Van Statten. 'An alien life form?'

'And you're quite sure it is alien? Because on initial inspection, I have to say I have doubts. This looks *designed.* Man-made. It is like a big pepperpot, yes? An alien that looks like a pepperpot, yes?'

Van Statten said, 'I want you to take a closer look.'

'Of course, of course,' said Kandinsky. 'I shan't be flown halfway around the world at a moment's notice without being fed and not take a closer look. Oh,' he said, and his voice was different, Van Statten was pleased at last to hear a note of surprise.

'What is it?'

'I thought this would be just a base metal. Tin, steel. I was wrong. There's a warmth to this. A texture I have never felt before.' He stroked at the pepperpot's casing. 'It's hard, this metal shell, but it also yields to the touch. It's like a skin.'

'Yes,' said Van Statten. 'Exactly.'

'But no,' Kandinsky went on, and he shook his head. 'Even in extraterrestrial conditions, why would Nature select such an unusual design? Its two arms at variant lengths. One like a sink plunger. The other, how you say, an egg whisk? It is preposterous.'

'And yet it is an alien creature,' said Van Statten softly. 'My alien creature.'

'Why have you chained it up?'

Goddard said, 'In case it moves.'

'And has it ever moved?'

Goddard said, 'No.' And Kandinsky threw her a withering look, and went back to his inspection of the casing. He inspected it for quite some time.

'Have you reached any sort of verdict, doctor? Doctor?'

The egg whisk twitched, and no one noticed.

'This is fascinating,' said Kandinsky. 'The longer I study it, the more contradictions I see. What can you tell me about where it comes from?'

'Not a thing,' said Van Statten. 'I was rather hoping the creature would tell us itself. I need you to get it talking.'

This at last made Kandinsky turn away from the pepperpot, and he looked at Van Statten in utter disbelief. 'Get it to do *what*?' he said. And he couldn't stop himself, he laughed.

'Sir, maybe it can't talk,' said Goddard. 'Maybe Duchesne was lying.'

And Van Statten rounded on her in sudden fury. 'Of course Duchesne was lying! I know Duchesne was lying! I am 99 per cent certain Duchesne was lying! But just in case. Just in case.' He turned back to Kandinsky. 'This is what you're here for, doctor. Make it talk for me, and we shall learn everything.'

Kandinsky was frightened of him now, Van Statten could see that, and was pleased. 'I'm sorry!' he babbled. 'But if this is alien, which I shall accept. And if this is a life form, which I shall entertain as a workable hypothesis. Then, still, you surely have to realise ...'

'What?' said Van Statten. 'Tell me what I *have* to do.'

'It's dead,' said Kandinsky. 'There's no life here.' And to demonstrate he rapped his knuckles on the skin-like metal; it gave a mournful clang.

'And that is your expert opinion, *doctor*?' sneered Van Statten. 'Maybe I should get another doctor, *doctor*.'

And maybe it was that word, 'doctor' – or maybe it was the contempt with which Van Statten said it. But in an instant everything changed, and for the rest of his life Dr Kandinsky's understanding of cosmology changed with it.

The scientist opened his mouth to reply, but instead looked back at the creature in sudden alarm. Alarm, and pain – his hand was still resting lightly upon its shell, and the shell was starting to glow.

Kandinsky screamed.

Goddard moved to help him, but Van Statten stopped her. 'Watch,' he said.

Kandinsky couldn't pull his hand away. He was tugging at it, but it wouldn't come free. And the harder he tried to break loose, the harder in return the metal skin seemed to pull back – the casing was sucking the hand in. And then the hand was lost, it was absorbed now, it was part of the alien monster. Not dead, not inert, but very much alive, and very *hungry* – Kandinsky was dragged in up to his wrist, and his scream now was terrible, it was inhuman, it was as inhuman as the beast that was feeding from him. The glow suddenly brightened, and Kandinsky at last, mercifully, fell silent. He began to shake. His feet tapped on the spot in fast frenzy, his free arm rising then falling against his flank, over and over again; it was some macabre dance, because Kandinsky was already dead, of course he was dead, his head rolled around the shoulders as his body juddered first this way then that. And he was glowing too, and he was burning, his whole body was burning. The man was on fire.

The creature gave out one sound – its cry was shrill. What was it? It was frustration. It was rage.

And then, suddenly, silence. The glowing just stopped, as if the power had been cut off. And Kandinsky's burned body dropped to the floor.

'It is alive,' whispered Henry Van Statten. 'I was right. Living creatures from beyond the stars.' His eyes were shining with tears of joy.

Goddard said, 'We're going to need another expert.'

5

The Doctor was already on the video screens outside the Cage, barking out orders. Rose noted that he'd already barged Van Statten out of the way, he was the one in charge. And yet as she watched him Rose felt such a sudden twinge in her stomach, and it took her a few seconds to realise why. She trusted the Doctor with her life. She'd seen him triumph over the odds a dozen times. But the Doctor on the screen was different. He was panicked. No, terrified.

'Keep the Dalek in that cell or we're all dead!' he was shouting.

And Bywater, the guard, was trying to calm him down, telling him the creature was locked within the Cage, there was no escape, the entry pad had a billion combinations. And the Doctor was shouting back, did they think a Dalek could be stopped by a *locked door*? It could calculate a hundred billion combinations in one second flat! They had to destroy it right now, before it got out, it was their only hope …

Rose wanted to explain that this was all her fault. The Doctor wasn't listening. 'Rose,' he yelled, 'just get out of there! Get out of there *now*!'

It was too late. The hum that the Cage door gave as it unlocked was insultingly bright and cheerful. The door swung open slow and unhurried.

'You've got to concentrate your fire!' said the Doctor.

'Don't damage it,' Van Statten said, 'I want it unharmed …' But if Van Statten had anything to add Rose couldn't hear it; the Dalek was now edging out of the cell, and Bywater and Klein were already shooting at it. The bullets hit the metal casing with a fierce scatter of sparks.

The Dalek stopped. It surveyed the room. It appeared to be *ignoring* the gunfire, it was a matter of supreme irrelevance. And then – then, at last, it found what it was looking for. The video screen. The Doctor's face filling it. And the Dalek made straight for it. Both the guards were forced to dodge out of the way.

The Dalek stared at the Doctor. The Doctor stared right back.

The Dalek raised its sucker arm. In greeting?

And then plunged it right through the screen, right through the Doctor's face.

The Dalek cried out as electricity arced around its body. But no longer was it being tortured – this time it was as if it were sucking the energy in, greedily taking every last scrap of it. The lights in the room began to flicker and dim.

'*We're losing power!*' Rose heard Goddard shout over Bywater's comms unit. '*I'm in Mr Van Statten's office and we have only one computer operational. What's going on?*'

Bywater snapped, 'Klein, take these civilians and get out of here. They are your responsibility, got that?' And without a word Klein nodded, swept Adam and Rose out into the corridor.

Goddard was still giving him orders, and Bywater knew he wasn't going to obey them. That he was on his own now. '*You too,*' she was telling him. '*Get out of there, take up a defensive position . . .!*'

'No,' said Bywater. 'I shall do my duty. Diana?'

A hesitation, as if Goddard had forgotten her own name. Then at last, quietly – '*Yes?*'

'You know I trust you to do yours. By any means necessary.' And then he began firing at the alien again, and he didn't hear any more.

Fifty-three floors above, just below the surface, the Doctor could more easily appreciate what the Dalek was doing. They were running on emergency lighting, only one single computer screen left glowing in Van Statten's office. Goddard was studying it with horror.

'It's drained the whole base,' she said. 'No, more than that. It's drained the power reserves for the whole of Utah.'

'It's not just power it's after,' said the Doctor. 'It's information. The Dalek is downloading the entire internet.'

'But that's impossible!'

'You have to admire it,' said Van Statten. He had been quiet all this while, sitting in his chair, lost in thought. The Doctor had thought he was in a state of panic, but his voice sounded now unnaturally calm. 'It makes the impossible possible. That's the way I've always lived, that's been my entire business model. We have so much in common.'

'It's coming to kill us,' said the Doctor.

'We have to protect it. We can seal it in the vaults. Lower the bulkhead doors. Trap it there until it has a chance to calm down.'

'You'd be trapping over a hundred staff down there with it!' said Goddard. Van Statten said nothing to this; he just smiled, and returned to his contemplation. Goddard turned to the Doctor. 'Tell me honestly,' she said. 'How dangerous is this creature really?'

The Doctor looked her in the eyes, and said slowly, 'Every single thing I have told you is true.'

And Goddard held his gaze. And nodded, and swallowed. She went to the comms unit. 'Emergency!' she announced. 'All guards to arm themselves, and convene at the Metaltron cage immediately!'

*

At last the Dalek disengaged from the Cage computer terminal.

It knew the truth.

It searched its neural pathways, looking for any information that might contradict it, offer up even some little ambiguity. Anything that might let it doubt what it had learned.

There was nothing.

The Dalek considered what it should do next.

It could simply stop. Let this be the death it had so long dreamed of. Put an end to the pain, and suffering, and all that dreadful hope.

It considered this rationally and cogently for the longest time. It considered this for several seconds.

'No,' it concluded. 'The Daleks survive. The Daleks survive *in me*!'

It fired its gun. It hadn't been able to do that for so many years, and it enjoyed the sensation as the laser bolts burst out of its body, and it could unleash all its hatred. Didn't it feel *good*? It fired at the computer. It fired at the walls and the ceiling and the doors. It fired over and over again, until the room was in flames.

The Dalek laughed. *It laughed.* Whatever would happen next – whether there could ever even be a next, for one last pointless survivor of a lost war – for the moment, at least, it felt free.

There was a sound that the Dalek struggled to identify. A pathetic little popping noise – and it turned, and realised that there, amidst the inferno, there stood one solitary human being, still shooting at it with its own gun. The bullets kept bouncing off its casing. It was irritating. It stung. But what really irked the Dalek wasn't so much the stinging, but that silly noise.

So the Dalek fired one last time, and then left the room.

For a Dalek, death itself is never a deterrent. Death is an essential part of existence. In most cases a death that is both well-timed and well-executed can be of great value to the welfare of the Dalek race. A duty to be embraced. Not something to be avoided – at worst, to be postponed.

So when the Daleks decided to unleash death upon creation, there was no strategic point in making that death painless. Daleks sought to deter all other life forms from being all other life forms – merely granting them the inevitability of extinction would teach them nothing. If there was a mercy to the killing, what would be the point in the killing at all?

Dalek scientists devised guns that did not merely kill, they would *exterminate*. To kill suggests something respectful; one rids the body of life, but at the end of the process it may still be recognisable. To exterminate is something altogether different. To destroy from within so completely that no trace will be no left, nothing that can be identifiable.

When a man is killed by a Dalek, the corpse still looks human. The physical shell is kept intact, because that makes it easier for when the bodies are cleared away en masse. But under the surface skin everything else has been scrambled. The heart, the lungs, the kidneys – the bones and all the blood cells – everything – all of it. Targeted by the Dalek laser bolt and burned away and reduced to a thick mulch. When a victim is caught in the blast of a Dalek gun, it is said that for a few seconds fellow soldiers can see their comrade's skeleton exposed, as if in the glare of a blazing X-ray, before it collapses in on itself and is turned to paste.

The Daleks do not think of this as a kindness. It is not within their scope of reason to think that anything is kind. But somewhere in their brains, very deep down, they think there is at least a straightforward honesty to the way in which they take lives. And to confer such honesty upon lower beings, that is a form of kindness, somehow, isn't it?

The dozen guards who responded to Goddard's call didn't know any of this, of course. They had all been recruited by Van Statten after years of active military service, and had since spent their lives parading around a secure base in uniform like toy soldiers for his pleasure. Some were eager for a bit of action.

Goddard told them that there was an alien life form that had to be terminated at all costs. They surrounded the Dalek on both sides outside the Cage, at the interchange of a corridor.

None of them had the rank to give orders – it simply wasn't in their job descriptions. They looked at each other hesitantly. One of them at last said, 'Fire at will!' and that seemed as good a plan as any.

The Dalek was too wide to turn in the corridor, but it swivelled its midsection, and began to shoot the guards down on all sides one by one. It seemed to have its own special order in which it had decided to kill them. Was it picking them off according to how much of a threat it assessed they individually posed? Or was it just having fun, keeping them guessing, letting them wonder which of them it would decide to destroy next?

And as the guards died, they heard Van Statten giving them urgent instructions over their comms units.

'Stop shooting at it! Do you hear me? I don't want a single scratch upon its bodywork! That creature is unique, and you are not. You are disposable! Lay down your guns this very second! Lay down your guns, or I'll have you sacked!'

Most of the soldiers didn't live long enough to hear the entirety of Van Statten's little speech, and the final man standing was too busy screaming as all his internal organs were displaced to feel especially offended.

6

This is the story of Maya Klein. It is not a remarkable story, and neither is it a happy one. But it won't take long to tell.

Maya met her husband Uri when they were both drafted to military service in Israel. She saw him on the very first day of training, and thought he was loud-mouthed, arrogant, and sort of weird-looking. Of course, she fell in love with him right away.

When they came out of the army they married. They had no money and no prospects, but they were young and didn't care. Uri became a car mechanic. 'We'll be fine,' he said, 'everyone will always need cars.' Maya got a job in a supermarket. They were both, in their own and very quiet ways, happy.

Then they had a baby son, and he made them happier still. Hours would go by when the two of them would just sit and stare at little Daniel. 'I wonder what his story will be,' Maya said. She knew she didn't have much of a story herself, she was so ordinary. But her baby son might grow up to be magnificent.

One day Uri asked if he could talk to his wife about something important. He looked so serious, and Uri never looked particularly serious. Right away, Maya was scared.

He explained that they weren't able to make ends meet. Both were borrowing money from their parents, but their parents weren't rich either, so what were they going to do? Uri said, 'I'm thinking of going back into service. I've had a letter. Look.'

He passed it to her, a letter on paper that was pure white, and crisp, and soft.

The letter summoned Uri to an interview the very next morning. There was a job on offer that could put his military training to good use, and he would be posted abroad for a period of three months. The letter said that he would be well rewarded.

It also said that all of this was strictly confidential, and he must not tell anyone under any circumstances.

The couple deliberated long into the night. They had their first major argument. But by morning they both agreed that, really, there was little choice. If not for their sakes, for Daniel – they needed the money, and three months wouldn't be too long. By the time Uri came back it would be spring, and the flowers would be out!

Uri came back from the interview angry. 'They wouldn't even see me,' he said. 'They told me I'd broken the confidentiality clause.'

'But how could they even know?' Maya said. 'I didn't tell anyone!' But Uri refused to speak to her for two days.

A week later Maya came home from the supermarket to find an envelope addressed to her waiting under the door. It was white, crisp and soft.

When she returned from her own interview, she told Uri she had to go away for a while, and that he mustn't ask questions. He would have to take care of Daniel on his own. 'Trust me,' she said. 'It will only be for three months.'

Maya had never dreamed she would ever visit America. For the first weeks of her contract she had to keep pinching herself, the idea was absurd. America was a concrete base under the Utah desert, with no natural light and only filtered air conditioning, but it was America nonetheless. It excited her.

She didn't know why she had been headhunted for this job. Her boss didn't so much as look at her. Until one day he pointed at her and said, 'You'll do. I need security detail for a meeting with the President.' She thought he must be joking, but together they flew in a helicopter; she was told she must not speak to the President, and Maya obliged and kept her mouth tightly shut. The President didn't appear to notice either way. On the flight home, having assumed she'd done her job efficiently, her boss told her flatly, 'You're not his type.' And from then on she was banished to guard duty at the museum on the 53rd floor.

Maya didn't mind. Her three months were nearly up. She missed her husband and her son more than she could find the words to say.

She only met her boss again on her final day. She was taken to his office. 'Thank you for your service,' he said. 'You may now return home. Or we can extend your contract for a further six months, and I'll double your pay. No, I'll quadruple it, why not?'

Maya felt her head swim. She explained that she needed to see her family, if only for a little while. The boss smiled. 'I'll give you the weekend.'

When Maya got back home she flew into Uri's arms. He wasn't angry with her. She thought he might have been. She didn't dare yet tell him she was leaving again so soon. Daniel was shy. He didn't want to hug her. He called her 'Mummy', but only because Uri told him to.

And that night Daniel refused to eat his dinner, so they had to punish him. Maya told him to sit upon the bottom step of the staircase, and that was the naughty step. Daniel didn't want to sit on the naughty step, and he cried, and said he was sorry. But Maya knew from her military training that a threat had no value unless you were prepared to carry it out, and she made him sit there for a whole ten minutes.

'He misses you,' said Uri. 'What do you expect?' He was trying so hard to be kind, it was the one time he let his impatience show.

'I'll be back soon,' she promised him. 'I can't tell you when. But it'll be soon.'

The next six months passed very slowly.

At the end of her term, she was once more summoned upstairs. This time her boss wasn't even there. Goddard had once been a guard, just the same as her; now she was Van Statten's second in command. Goddard told Maya that Mr Van Statten wanted to extend her contract once more, this time for a period of two years. And Maya began to say no, but the sum of money now being offered was astronomical, and she knew she could never turn it down.

'But what does he want me for?' asked Maya, and she was crying, she couldn't help it. 'What's the point?'

Goddard didn't say anything, but gave as sympathetic a shrug as possible. And Maya understood that both of them were equally subject to the whims of a wealthy sociopath.

This time, she was allowed just one night with her family.

Their home had a brand new widescreen television; Maya was pleased that the money she earned was being put to good use. Uri looked different. He had lost weight. He'd grown a trim beard. 'You can't expect things to stay the same,' he said. She wondered if he were seeing anyone else, and decided not to ask.

And Daniel was no longer shy with her; he was furious. He wouldn't go near her. He swore at her. 'It's the naughty step for you, young man!' Maya said, and he said no. She told him that if he didn't sit on the naughty step she'd be forced to punish him further, and he said he didn't bloody care. And a soldier has to follow through on her threats or you look weak, so she slapped him.

It was only a gentle slap, but as soon as she had done it she wanted to take it back. 'I'm sorry, baby,' she said, and she tried to put her arms around him. Daniel pushed her away. He stomped over to the naughty step, and sat down upon it hard. And he refused to move from it, his red face hot with angry tears, he refused to speak to her again, and at last Uri had to pick him up and carry him to bed.

When Bywater instructed Maya at the Cage to get Rose and Adam to safety, she was pleased. It was a purpose she understood – she would protect the civilians. And as they ran through the corridors of the 53rd floor, with the Dalek in pursuit, she kept the rear at all times – even though she knew they weren't running fast enough, that they weren't trained for action as she was.

She felt strangely happy.

They reached the staircase. With no power for the lifts, it was half a mile of stairs straight up – Maya knew that her charges weren't fit enough to do that at speed, she wasn't sure she would be. But there was no time to lose, and she ushered them onwards, wished that they could pick up the pace, would take two steps at a time.

'Look!' Adam called. He had stopped. Why had he stopped? They had to keep moving. In spite of herself, Maya stopped too, and dared to look behind her.

The Dalek had reached the bottom of the stairwell. It bumped against the step. It backed up, moved forward once more – bumped back into the step again. Like a housefly unable to work out why it can't get through a pane of glass.

Adam jeered. 'Great big alien death machine, defeated by a flight of stairs!' He actually dared to laugh out loud.

The Dalek fixed him with its gaze, then let the eyestalk droop disconsolately so it could watch itself, one last time, bump back into that step. It was almost comical.

'Elevate,' it intoned quietly, and its base began to glow, it began to hover, it began to *fly*.

Adam had the sense to stop laughing.

'Get out of here, keep running,' Maya said to her two charges. It was the first time they had heard her voice.

'We can't just leave you here!' the girl said. 'You can't stop it!' The girl was concerned for her. That was kind.

'It's my job to try,' said Maya, simply. 'Just go.' And Adam was already running, he was out of sight. Maya didn't blame him. The girl began running after.

Maya Klein stared down at the Dalek as it slowly glided up the stairs towards her. Her gun was drawn. She didn't remember drawing it. 'Stop,' she said.

And, incredibly, the Dalek did. It stopped to listen to what she had to say.

Maya tried to find the words.

'Listen,' she said. 'I demand that you surrender. If you want to negotiate, then I guarantee we shall be willing to discuss terms. But the killing has to stop. You must surrender right now.' It seemed to her that the Dalek was hovering on the naughty step.

The Dalek interrupted her. 'You are a soldier.'

'Yes,' she said.

'You are bred to receive orders,' it said. 'You do not have the authority to negotiate.'

'That's right,' said Maya. 'I am just a soldier.'

The Dalek seemed to consider this. 'We are the same,' it said. And was there some fellow feeling in that, she wondered.

'It's not fair,' she said quietly.

The Dalek did not contradict her.

It moved off the naughty step. It wasn't allowed to do that. Maya fired her gun. A soldier must – no, a *mother* must follow through on her threats. She fired the gun over and over again.

Up until the last moments, Maya Klein thought she might still be able to persuade the Dalek to stop, and to sit back down upon the naughty step.

This is the end of her story. She will not be mentioned again.

7

'Everything in the museum is electronically tagged, so we can see the Dalek here. It's already reached level 50.'

Goddard was showing the Doctor the schematic of the base on the computer. The Doctor wondered whether she had realised how quietly and effectively she had taken control. He wondered whether Van Statten had either – and decided he probably hadn't. 'Are there any alien weapons in the collection?' he asked.

'Oh, plenty!' said Van Statten, and laughed.

'The trouble is,' Goddard said tersely, 'the Dalek happens to be between us and them.'

The Doctor pointed out a large blank area on the screen. 'And here, what's this at level 46?'

'Weapons testing area.'

'The Dalek will have to pass through it. It's the perfect place for an ambush. Give guns to everyone – the soldiers, the technicians, the lawyers. It's the only chance we have to take it out.'

Goddard nodded. 'I'm on it.'

Van Statten said lazily, 'I think you're going about this whole thing the wrong way.'

'And why is that?' the Doctor asked absently, as he continued to study the screen.

'My father was a businessman. Smartest one I ever knew. He taught me that the only way to overcome insuperable odds is to make them work *for* you. If you can't defeat the enemy, do a merger.'

Goddard said, 'You've been torturing it for years. Do you think you can negotiate with it now?'

Van Statten stroked his neat, trim beard. 'I've had business rivals who would happily have seen me killed a hundred times over. But revenge is only ever a single motivating factor, and as soon as you get around the conference table, you'll always find there are better ones. All we need to do is find out what the Dalek *wants*. Everything wants something. That's its weakness.'

'Oh, Van Statten,' said the Doctor. 'You are so right. It wants something, yeah.'

'Then tell me what. You're the great expert. Prove your worth.'

'I wish it were revenge. Revenge would be so simple. We'd be laughing, if it were just revenge.'

'How so?'

'Because then,' said the Doctor, 'we'd all die, and once it had killed us, the Dalek might stop. But the Dalek won't stop. Not ever. What's the nearest city?'

Van Statten looked thrown. 'Salt Lake City.'

'Population?'

'A quarter million.'

'All dead. Every last one of them. When the Dalek gets out, it'll murder every living creature. *That's* what it wants. Try getting that discussed around your conference table.'

Unnerved at last, Van Statten snapped, 'But why would it do that?'

'Because it honestly believes they should die. Human beings are different, and different is wrong. It's the ultimate in racial cleansing, and you, Van Statten, have let it loose!'

Van Statten said uneasily, 'I refuse to believe that.'

'You still think there's a way out of this, don't you? You're finished. We're all finished. This is what you've done. You've killed us all. And the most we can do, the best we can hope for, is that we don't take the rest of the world with us.'

Goddard looked up from the comms unit. She said, 'The commander is ready, Doctor, do you have any instructions?'

'Unless,' said the Doctor, ignoring her, 'we take this *one* chance, this one last chance, and hold it off here. Unless we get *very* lucky. So you just hope, Van Statten. While all the people braver than you pick up their guns and go to war.' He went to the comms unit and spoke into it. 'Listen to me,' he said. 'I can get you through this, but you need to do exactly what I say.'

*

On the 46th floor, the staircase opened onto a corridor that led at last to a reception area. 'The main stairwell picks up from along here' panted Adam. 'This way!' He did not look especially fit, but he was running fast – it was astonishing how sheer terror could turn even the weakest of men into an athlete. As for Rose, she was exhausted. It was a relief to be running on a flat surface again, but her ankles hadn't adjusted, the way they didn't if she spent a night out too long in high heels. She kept thinking how she might trip over herself. *Stop thinking of that*, she told herself. *Stop thinking, and run. And* don't *trip*.

Because the Dalek had to be right behind them. There was a faint hum in the air, and Rose couldn't be sure, maybe it was just noise from the air conditioning – but she thought it might well be the sound of the Dalek hovering up the stairs. It was wiser to think it might be the Dalek. Just keep moving.

Rose and Adam rounded a corridor, and suddenly they were blinded by a bright light. And she froze, rabbit in the headlights. She felt Adam freeze beside her.

For an instant she thought, *Is this death? Have I been shot from behind?*

That would almost be a relief. You're it. Game over. You lost.

And then she heard a voice shouting at them. 'What are you doing? Get out of there! Hold your fire!' And the lights were dimming a bit, or perhaps she was just getting used to the brightness, and she saw great lamps had been turned upon them, and all around there were men and women with guns, some on the ground, some on the upper gantries. In guard uniform, in lab coats, in smart business suits.

'Get *out* of there!' the voice yelled once more, and that broke her paralysis – she was running again, and Adam was running too. Through this rag-tag band of soldiers, to safety.

'It's here! It's here!' someone else screamed in panic, and the commander once more shouted orders. Take positions, everyone – wait for the signal – and for God's sake, *hold your fire*. And Rose realised just how close behind them the Dalek had been after all.

She stopped dead.

'Come on!' urged Adam. 'Don't stop, why have you stopped?'

Rose didn't know. Her legs wouldn't move. It wasn't exhaustion. It was if they no longer belonged to her.

She turned her head around.

On the other side of the room, maybe a hundred metres away, the Dalek was facing her.

It was looking at her.

At her, and no one else. She could feel it in her mind. As if it knew her. As if it *wanted* to know her, more than anything else in the world.

As if it dreaded knowing her, but it had no choice.

'Open fire!' she heard, and at once everyone began to shoot.

The Dalek didn't seem to notice. It maintained its position, staring across at her. As if the battle was of no interest whatsoever.

Rose felt Adam tugging her arm, and she wanted to tell him to get off her, to leave them alone, *to leave them both alone* – and it took the greatest effort to turn her head to shout at him, and there he was, and he looked so frightened and confused, and that seemed to release something. There was life back in her legs, she could *move*.

'Please,' said Adam. 'I don't want to leave you.' And he took her by the hand, and he pulled her along, and her own legs began to cooperate, as if they at last recalled what they had to do.

She was free, and running once more. And yet there was a voice in her head, something she could only dimly hear: *Next time I see you, I shall kill you.*

To start with, they remembered what the Doctor had told them.

'Concentrate your fire,' he had said. 'The Dalek's battle armour is strong, but it is not indestructible. Aim for the dome, the head, that's the weak spot. Aim for the eyepiece.'

So that's what they had done, at first.

Eighty-nine people with guns, most of whom had never been trained for combat, most of whom had never even *held* a gun before. Firing upon a creature that didn't even retaliate.

The Dalek stared after Rose, as if lost in a dream.

And it's so easy to shoot at an enemy that doesn't bother to shoot back. You know what? – it's *fun*. The accountants and the lawyers began to whoop and jeer. Some of them stepped out of cover, pretended they were Rambo, pretended they were in the movies.

The impact of all those bullets was blasting the Dalek up against the far wall. And, at last, it even toppled sideways on to the floor. A cheer went up! The battle was all but won.

Rose Tyler had gone. It would think about her later.

The Dalek made a decision.

In Van Statten's office all the video screens switched on, each of them showing what was taking place on level 46.

'We've got power back!' said Goddard.

'The Dalek is doing this,' said the Doctor. 'It wants us to see.'

The Dalek righted itself, but what of that?

It began to hover in the air. But really, what of that either? If anything, it made it an easier target.

The soldiers continued to cheer. The creature was trying to escape by flying away! But there was nowhere for it to fly to, couldn't it see that? Not with a concrete ceiling, and 45 floors above it. It was trapped. The stupid creature, it was scared. Let's put it out of its misery.

They shot uselessly at its base skirting, and at its midsection. Some of them were even shooting straight into the air now, just for fun.

The first laser bolt the Dalek fired took out the electrical cables. They sparked, then burst into flames. And immediately all the sprinklers in the room were activated, pouring out tons of water to douse the fire.

That was all the Dalek needed to do for a while. It waited patiently.

The Doctor watched the Dalek bask in the fall of rain, its eyestalk raised in what seemed like joy, the water bouncing off its casing. The Doctor thought it looked ecstatic.

By now the soldiers were all standing ankle-deep in the wet. Even drenched, nothing could dampen their enthusiasm. Most of them were still cheering when the Dalek fired its second laser bolt straight down at the ground. Down at the water lapping around their feet.

It was the soldiers on the gantries who were given a few seconds to panic. They were just in time to see all their comrades beneath them writhe and contort as they were electrocuted. 'Fall back!' cried the commander. But there really wasn't time to fall back, not when the gantries were just as soaking wet as the ground level, not when the Dalek had one more laser bolt to send.

They were all dead. The brave heroes of the battle of the 46th floor. Eighty-nine corpses lying twisted and burned, and still the water continued to fall.

The Dalek stared directly down the camera lens, just so the Doctor could see. Then it flicked its eyestalk just a fraction – what was that, a *shrug*? And it turned off the video screens.

There was a stunned silence in the office.

Van Statten said quietly, 'I think perhaps a new strategy is in order. Goddard, prepare the helicopter. I shall vacate the base.'

'But there's no power to the helipad,' said Goddard.

'Then I shall go there myself,' said Van Statten. 'Operate it manually. Yes.'

'There isn't even enough power for the lift. You can't get to the surface.'

Van Statten began to walk the room, to shake his head. 'No,' he said. 'No, no, no. We're all going to die. What you said, you were right. We're all going to die.'

And he pulled a gun from his desk, and pointed it at the Doctor.

'The Dalek wants you dead, yes. Maybe if I were to give you to the Dalek ...'

The Doctor didn't even raise his voice. 'I'm sure it'd thank you very nicely. Just before it exterminated you.'

'It's still a chance.'

'No, Van Statten! The *only* chance you've got is me. I am the only person who can possibly stop it.'

'Put the gun down,' said Goddard.

Van Statten ignored her. 'And exactly how will you stop it, Doctor? Please, convince me. I am a reasonable man. You can see I'm being a reasonable man.'

The Doctor interrupted him. 'I don't know yet.'

Van Statten seemed to consider this, just for a moment, as if it were a workable business proposition, as if it were something he could bring up before the shareholders and the board. Then he shook his head with a smile. 'No, not good enough,' he said, and he cocked the trigger. And the Doctor wondered whether he would shoot him then and there, Dalek or no Dalek.

'I said,' Goddard repeated, 'put the gun down.' The Doctor and Van Statten turned to her, and saw that she had drawn a gun of her own.

'What is this?' said Van Statten weakly.

'I am a federal agent,' said Goddard. 'Put down your weapon. You have the right to remain silent.'

Van Statten burst into laughter. 'You're choosing this moment to *arrest* me?'

And Goddard came closer, pushed the gun right up against Van Statten's head, hard. 'Or maybe we just give you to the Dalek. Let's see what it does with *you*.'

'Enough of this,' said the Doctor. 'I know you're scared, but this is pathetic. If you want to survive, either of you – then you have to be better than this.'

And then he realised that neither of them were even listening. Both were staring at the video screen. Both, dazedly, lowering their guns.

The screen was back on, and the Dalek filled it. 'I shall speak only to the Doctor,' it said.

The Agent's Tale

Henry Van Statten had had three wives, and each time he'd got married he'd done so with a decreasing sense of curiosity. With his first wife he'd actually been quite interested to see what might happen; by wife number three he had to admit to himself he was largely doing it all out of habit. On the honeymoon she had said to him, 'You need to decide what's more important! There's only room in your life for your alien collection, or me!' And Henry had listened to her, and agreed with her, and thanked her for her good counsel. And made sure he wiped her mind very gently before depositing her on the side of the road.

It wasn't that he disliked women. He just didn't find them particularly relevant. He didn't find men particularly relevant either but, he supposed, biologically speaking at least, he shared certain things in common with them. If he *had* to surround himself with people (and he knew he did – the scientists, the accountants, all the guards with their guns) then they might as well be male.

But he did employ a few women. He had no weakness for them himself, but he knew that most of his business associates did, and any weakness was useful to exploit.

One day Van Statten decided it was high time he paid another visit to the President of the United States, and he knew the President had an *especial* weakness for women. Straight away he went to see whether there were any female guards on duty. There was just the one – he knew she was efficient, severe, and quite possibly beautiful.

'You'll do,' he said to her.

In the helicopter he told the guard her duties. 'You're there to be seen. Don't speak unless you're spoken to. In fact, don't speak even if you are spoken to. I'm not going to want to hear your voice, and I don't care whether the President does.'

'Yes, sir,' she said, short, to the point.

'Now, this is going to be a long flight, and I should like to pretend you're not here.' There wasn't much room in the helicopter, but she did her very best to accommodate his wishes, and tried to make herself as small as possible.

At last they began their descent over a golf course in Florida. Sand was blown all over the very lush, very green grass; they all but emptied one of the bunkers. Secret service agents ran up to the helicopter, pistols drawn. Van Statten said, 'At ease, boys. Well done, that was impressive. Now, I want to be alone with the President, why don't you all go off and grab a beer?' And the secret servicemen relaxed, and put away their guns, and wandered off to the clubhouse – because they'd pledged to keep the President safe from all threats, but only so long as Henry Van Statten told them to.

She thought the President looked much shorter and fatter than he did on the television. He bounded up like a puppy dog, nervous, eager to please. 'Mr Van Statten! What a wonderful surprise! If you had only let me know ...'

'I like to keep you on your toes,' said Van Statten.

'Of course, of course!' The President laughed, and even jumped around on those toes for a bit, to prove that he got the joke. He looked at the female guard and smiled; he even licked his lips slightly. 'And what is your name?' he asked.

'Eyes front, Mr President,' said Van Statten. 'Listen to me. You're tanking in the polls. You're ten points down. The whole point of keeping you in power is to make the people think they're happy. Otherwise, what do I need you for?'

The President said, 'I'm trying very hard, sir. The polls say I'm making some of the people happy.'

'Yes.'

'But by making *those* people happy, I end up making lots of others *extremely* unhappy. It's so difficult getting the balance right.'

'I'll tell you what,' said Van Statten. 'It's a beautiful day. And we're on this beautiful golf course. And you like golf, don't you, Mr President?'

'It's the only way I can make the nightmares stop.'

'Then this is what we'll do. We'll play a round of golf together, you and I. Who knows, you might even beat me! And if you do, you can still be President this time tomorrow.'

'Yes, sir. Thank you, sir,' said the President. 'Thank you for the opportunity.'

And that's how they spent the next few hours – Henry Van Statten and the leader of the free world, striking at balls for fun. They seemed well matched. Sometimes Van Statten would get a hole in one, and that made the President get scared – but then, unaccountably, at the next hole he'd hit the ball in the wrong direction altogether, and the President was able to even the score. Van Statten was highly amused by the game; the President, in contrast, was desperate to please.

The guard caddied for Van Statten. She would have caddied for the President too, but Van Statten told her he could carry his own damned clubs – and he huffed and puffed his way around the course, his fat face scarlet with the effort, his expensive toupee slick with sweat.

They reached the final, 18th hole. 'It all comes down to this one, Mr President,' said Van Statten, and smiled. 'Good luck!' The President made a strange and incoherent little gibbering noise, and swung with his club – he missed the ball, and again, and again. 'Please,' he said. 'I love my job.' And when Van Statten said nothing, he turned to the guard – he actually grabbed hold of her arm – he actually began to cry. 'Put in a good word,' he said. 'Help me. Help me.'

The guard spoke for the first time. 'Mr Van Statten knows best,' she said.

The President froze – he realised he'd gone too far. And the guard froze too – she'd disobeyed a direct order. Both of them slowly turned to see how Van Statten might react.

And he was laughing. 'Oh, come now!' he said. 'Don't be upset, Mr President. Of course your position is secure. If you really promise you'll try harder. If you really promise, next time we play golf, that you'll up your game.'

'I do promise!' the President said, and now he was laughing too, in such relief. 'I promise anything! Thank you, thank you!'

'Then don't you worry,' said Van Statten. 'After all, what would the world do without you?'

On the flight back to the base, the guard didn't know whether Van Statten would rebuke her for speaking out of turn, or simply ignore her and expect her to be small and discreet once more. Instead he growled, 'So, who shall we replace him with? A Republican or a Democrat?'

The guard said, without thinking, 'Democrat, sir.'

Van Statten's fierce little eyes flashed. 'Why?'

'Because … they're just so funny, sir.'

Van Statten stared at her, and she realised that for the first time he was genuinely considering her, turning the whole weight of his power and cold intellect upon her and seeing whether she would squirm. She knew she mustn't squirm. She didn't.

'What's your name?' he said.

'Diana Goddard.'

'I like you, Diana Goddard. How would you like to be my chief of staff?'

And that's how Diana became second in command to the most powerful man in America.

On her seventh birthday Diana was informed that her father had been killed in the line of duty. He had been a cop – nothing special, nothing high ranked, just an ordinary cop. And it wasn't even true – he'd in fact been off duty at the time, on his way home to his daughter's party, and he had chosen the wrong time to intervene in a dispute on the subway.

They told her that her father had been a hero. 'He died to make the world a better place.' Diana tried to believe that, she really did. But it was hard to think of Pop as a hero, that shy awkward man who never liked to hug her, who only muttered that he loved her as if the words embarrassed him. Who spent all of his time at work.

How had his death made the world a better place? She didn't have a father any longer. And her mommy was sad, she cried so much, she cried sometimes for days on end. How was that in any way better?

She hated him. She loved him. She decided she would follow in his footsteps, she too would become a cop. Her mother tried to talk her out of it, but her mother was never strong enough to get her own way.

Diana excelled at school, and at 18 was told she'd be wasted as a cop. If she really wanted to be of service to her country, she should be fast-tracked to the FBI. And Diana did briefly wonder whether that would be a betrayal of her father, and what he had lived for, and what he had died for. But the truth was sadly simple. She could now barely remember him, and the only mental image of Pop she had left was from the wedding photograph her mother still resolutely kept in their kitchen at home. She could be better than him. She could let go.

On her first day training at Quantico she met her tutor, a burly Chicago Irishman called Owen Bywater. He asked her why she wanted to be a federal agent.

'To make the world a better place,' she said.

He laughed at her, and told her she was very naïve.

They became lovers.

They kept the relationship discreet. On Sundays they would get together, and lie next to each other in bed, and he would generously share with her his experience of 15 years' service as an operative in the field. Diana listened to what he said, and some things she accepted, and some things she did not.

One day he said, 'If there was a man you knew had committed a terrible crime, and you had the evidence to put him away, would you use it?'

'Of course,' said Diana.

'But what if you knew there was even better evidence out there? Even more damning. That would put him away for much longer. Would you keep quiet for the greater good? Would you let him continue his crimes, and be patient?'

Diana thought about it. 'I don't know.'

'Not knowing is the wrong answer,' said Bywater. 'You'll have to know.' And then they didn't talk about it again.

Diana graduated with flying colours, and after the ceremony she received a message to see Bywater privately. She was irritated; she would rather have celebrated with her friends. She went to see him.

'Congratulations,' he said, and kissed her.

'Thanks.'

'I'm about to leave, the agency are putting me back in the field. There's an opportunity to bring down a real bad guy. Someone we know who's very powerful, and very dirty.'

'Well done.'

'I'll be going undercover. I'd like to bring you in with me. I know you're just a rookie, but I believe you're the most promising agent I have had in years, and I have taught you everything I know. Would you be my right-hand man? Gathering information. Being patient. Bringing him down, by any means necessary.'

'By any means necessary,' said Diana. 'Thank you. Sir.' And absurdly she didn't know what he expected her to do – kiss him, or shake his hand, or, what, salute?

He could see the difficulty she was in. 'For the duration of the assignment, I think it's best our relationship is placed on hold.'

'I have no problem with that at all,' she said.

They worked at the Van Statten base, Bywater as security chief, Diana as a menial guard. They avoided all unnecessary contact, only meeting in the lower vaults when either one activated a coded password.

The day Diana flew back from her golf course encounter with the President, she summoned Bywater with the most urgent coded password they had. They met on the covered stairwell on level 55.

Bywater listened quietly as Diana explained the new situation. He didn't speak for a while. Then he said, 'Such direct exposure to the target. It might be wiser to pull you out right now before the operation is compromised.'

'No,' said Diana. 'I've already accepted.'

'Without clearing it with me? Why?'

‘Van Statten is a man of whim. The whim was the whole point. Don’t think the job would still be available if I’d hesitated even for a moment.’

‘You’re right, of course,’ said Bywater. ‘But it’s such a risk.’ Irritably he slammed his hand against the wall, and she watched him, this man she had once found impressive, this man she had wondered whether she loved. When had he become so timid?

‘Risk,’ she said. ‘Or opportunity. Van Statten doesn’t respect me. But that’s his biggest flaw. I’m a woman. He’ll underestimate me in a way he’d never underestimate you.’

‘I’m not happy about it.’

‘But it’s done.’

Bywater nodded unhappily. ‘By any means necessary. Promise you’ll take care of yourself?’

Diana said, ‘And I’m going to demote you. Security chief is no longer suitable, it’s too exposed. You can have my old job. You can be an ordinary guard. I’ll have you assigned to the Cage.’

‘That makes sense,’ said Bywater. ‘Yes, you’ll have to pretend to be my superior for the while. But don’t forget, this is still my operation, right? You take your orders from me.’

‘Always,’ said Diana Goddard.

Goddard stared down at the blackened corpse of Dr Kandinsky, still smouldering at her feet. She thought she was going to gag, but she fought her feelings down – oh, she'd got so good at fighting her feelings down since she'd started working for Henry Van Statten. She heard herself say, 'We're going to need another expert.' It sounded properly cold, and dispassionate, and dead.

Van Statten said, 'I think I've been looking for the wrong type of expert. We don't need some scientist, but a man of force. All we need to do is make it *talk*.' Without even a glance back at the dead body, he left the Cage.

Goddard called in a guard. By chance, it was Bywater. She started upon realising it was him, just for a second. She said, 'Take out this body and get rid of it.'

Bywater tried his hardest to look dispassionate too. It annoyed Goddard that by now she was better at that than he was. 'Right away, ma'am,' he said.

She hissed, 'We have to put an end to this.'

And Bywater seemed frightened, and he looked all about him, as if there were hidden cameras everywhere, and there were. 'Not now. We'll discuss this later.'

'No,' she said. 'Now. We discuss it now. There's a man killed, what more evidence do you need ... ?'

'It's the wrong sort of evidence ...'

'Don't you dare tell me that ...'

'I've gained access to his tax returns, you must be patient ...'

'And don't you *dare* tell me to be patient!' She knew she was shouting now, and that was so dangerous, but she didn't care – all the pent-up fury she'd contained while working undercover was released. This was wrong, he had to know this was wrong, and they *weren't* making the world a better place, they were so very, very far from making the world a better place. Her Pop would be ashamed.

Bywater was staring at her, appalled and embarrassed, and she waited for him to say anything useful – a promise that things would be put right, an apology even, something. Something that would justify her years of training. But he didn't make a sound. Except – there was a metallic rasp. It seemed almost like laughter. And it wasn't coming from Bywater. He had moved his head in the direction of the sound; she did the same.

The pepperpot laughed at them, and then fell silent.

'It's alive,' said Bywater.

'That metal creature is the last of our problems,' said Goddard. 'This has to end soon. One way or the other.' And she turned her back on them both, and walked away.

8

So the Doctor and the Dalek talked.

The Doctor watched it on the screens in Van Statten's office. Hovering high over the corpses, water still raining down hard upon its casing, it stared out at him in defiance. The Doctor thought he had never seen a Dalek look so magnificent. He felt a curious urge to tell it that. He fought it down..

Instead he said, 'You're going to get rusty.'

'I have fed off Rose Tyler,' the Dalek told him. 'She carries the energy from within your TARDIS that allows the Time Lords to regenerate. Now I too am new born.'

'And what's your next trick?'

'I have been searching for the Daleks.'

'Yeah, I saw. Downloading the internet. Wading through a lot of bare bodies, and petitions for the revival of *Buffy the Vampire Slayer*.'

'All irrelevance has been disposed of,' said the Dalek flatly. 'I have scanned the satellites and radio telescopes. Searching for any signal from the Dalek race.'

'And?'

'Nothing.'

The Dalek fell silent. It fell silent for a long time, and the Doctor wondered whether it would speak again. Then suddenly it cried out, loud and plaintive.

'*Where shall I get my orders now?*'

'You're just a soldier without commands,' the Doctor said, and at that the Dalek seemed to droop.

But just for a second. It raised its eyestalk, and spoke with fresh defiance. 'Then I shall follow the Primary Directive. The Dalek instinct to destroy.'

'But what for? Can't you see? It's all gone. Everything you were, everything you stood for.'

'Yes,' said the Dalek softly. 'It is all over.'

'So let it end. Just let it end. There is no point any more, not to any of this.' The Doctor was pleading now. Pleading with a Dalek, it embarrassed him. It made him feel dirty and small. 'You're the last. There's no point to *you*.'

'And no point to you either, Doctor.'

'Yeah,' said the Doctor. 'Yeah, and maybe that's true too.'

The Dalek seemed to consider this.

'Then what must I do?' it asked. 'If I have to give myself orders, what orders must I give?'

'You want me to help you.'

'You are the only creature that knows the Daleks. Tell me what I must do.'

'All right,' said the Doctor. 'If you want orders, here's an order. Kill yourself.'

'But the Daleks must survive.'

'The Daleks have failed! So why don't you just finish the job? Make the Daleks extinct. Rid the universe of your filth! Why don't you just *die*?' And the Doctor realised he was shouting – no, he was raging, he was screaming straight at the video screen.

He stopped himself.

The Dalek stared at him.

There was no judgement in the Dalek's response. But there was a new hard certainty, the doubts were gone. 'You would make a good Dalek.'

And then the screens went blank.

The Doctor took one breath, then another. He could sense Van Statten and Goddard behind him, watching all the while – watching as he'd failed to negotiate, to save all their lives. He said quietly, 'Seal the vaults.'

The bulkheads on the 40th floor were two metres thick, and were made out of corrugated steel. Once lowered, they cut off the lower depths of the base entirely from the outside world. They had been designed to protect Van Statten in the event of a nuclear war.

In recent years Van Statten had grown less concerned about some nebulous apocalypse. If there were ever to be Armageddon at any point, he was quite certain it wouldn't be triggered without his approval. And yet, he was drawn to these bulkheads. To the dream that he could one day just seal himself off, forever and completely – these thick doors would come crashing down, and from that point on he would be alone in his own private universe. No more business meetings, or mergers, or corporate coups. No more people. Just him, and his alien collection.

He wished he could be all alone now. That he could just be locked away, and nothing would ever get at him again, and he would have peace.

Dimly he listened to Goddard arguing with the Doctor. 'But the bulkheads are massive, we simply don't have the power to lower them!'

'There's emergency power,' said the Doctor. 'We just have to reroute it.'

'The Dalek is on the move – it's already reached the 45th floor! There's no time! You'd have to bypass the security codes, it would take a computer genius!'

'Lucky you've got me, then,' said Van Statten.

'You want to help?' said the Doctor.

'Yes,' said Van Statten. 'I want to help.' He took the chair at the computer from the Doctor. 'Nobody knows this software better than me.'

'You're still under arrest,' said Goddard, and Van Statten laughed. He began to tap at the computer. The screen filled with protocols, they danced before his eyes

– and his fingers on the keyboard danced with them. He would leech power off the ground defences, he could reduce the lighting and the oxygen supply.

'Can you do it?' the Doctor asked.

'No idea, let's find out, shall we? I haven't had to work so hard in years!' And he laughed again. This was good, this was *fun*.

'Doctor,' said Goddard. 'Your friend is still down there.'

Stairs ahead of her, stairs behind her, and Rose was running, she was always running. Adam just ahead of her, and concrete all about, and she knew in her heart she'd never see daylight again, not if she ever dared stop *running*. She wasn't even thinking any more, thinking might slow her down, she was just putting all her trust in her legs and hoping they wouldn't betray her. When she heard her phone ring she actually pulled it out to answer it, and her dazed brain began to yell at her, *What do you think you're doing? Not now! Keep running! Run! Run!* 'Sorry,' said Rose, 'this really isn't a good time ...'

It was the Doctor. 'Rose, where are you?'

'Level 43 ...'

'You've got to keep moving! Listen to me! They're going to seal off the vaults at level 40. If you don't get out, you'll die!'

'Can't you stop them? Doctor? ... Doctor!'

And the Doctor spoke again, and this time his voice was colder. '*I'm* sealing off the vaults. I won't wait, and I won't help you. For God's sake, run.'

'I've done it!' Van Statten actually yelped in surprise. He was good. Oh, he used to be so *good*, why couldn't he be good any longer? 'Power through to the bulkheads. We need to lower them now.'

'Just another couple of minutes,' said the Doctor. 'Give her as much time as we can.'

'No, we don't have any time! The power is already fluctuating, I won't be able to keep hold of it!'

Goddard was following the Dalek's progress. 'It's right behind them.'

Van Statten cried, 'If you don't lower them, I'll do it myself!'

'No,' said the Doctor. 'I'll do it. It has to be me.'

One single tap on the keyboard, and the bulkheads would start to lower.

He'd sacrificed his own race. He'd sacrificed everything he'd thought he was, what had made him the Doctor. His own conscience. What would that all count for now, if at the final throw of the dice, he couldn't sacrifice his best friend into the bargain? A human girl. Just a human girl.

Do it, Doctor. Damn yourself completely.

So this was who he was. He couldn't escape it after all.

'I'm sorry,' he said, although he wasn't really sure to whom.

He pressed the key.

They had reached the 40th floor at last, and were racing down one of the interminable concrete corridors. Adam was ahead – the Dalek, she knew, was close behind. She could *feel* it now, still looking at her, still trying to work out what she was. And a hundred metres ahead, the bulkhead door was closing.

Adam was through. Adam was safe. She would be safe too. It was closing so slowly – it was groaning under its sheer weight – she would make it out in time.

She felt another pull at her legs.

No, she thought. *No!*

She forced herself to run on, but her legs were jerking now, she was starting to stumble.

Let go! she screamed at the creature inside her head.

'Adam!' she cried. 'Help me!'

And she could see Adam hesitate – he turned around and stopped – could he dive back under the bulkhead door in time, pull her along, get back to safety?

He didn't say anything. His face aghast.

Still, she limped on. She could make it. She could squeeze under.

She could no longer squeeze under. She couldn't make it.

She turned around. She looked at the Dalek, and it was so much closer than she'd feared.

The bulkhead was sealed. And straight away the Doctor was on the phone – 'Rose? Where are you? Did you make it?'

He heard her voice. 'I'm sorry,' she said.

'Rose,' he said. 'Rose.' He didn't know what to say next.

'It's not your fault,' she said, although it was. 'Doctor, listen …' And then he heard the Dalek give its battle cry, and there was a laser bolt, and it had killed her, it had *exterminated* her, and the phone was just static now, there was nothing more to be heard.

He closed his eyes, and tried to bury himself in the silence.

Van Statten's voice dragged him back to the world. 'I'm sorry,' he dared to say.

'You're sorry?' asked the Doctor quietly. 'I could have killed that Dalek in its cell, but you stopped me.'

'It was the prize of my collection …'

'Your *collection*?' And the Doctor was advancing on Van Statten, his hands clenched tight into fists, and the man was backing away. 'Was it worth it? Worth all those men's lives? Worth Rose? I said I'd protect her. She was only here because of me.' And he was sweeping

Van Statten's desk bare, all the little alien artefacts, the space rocks, the spaceship hubcaps, all the rubbish, all the useless *junk*. Worthless, worthless. A child's telescope now smashed upon the floor.

'Let me tell you something, Van Statten,' said the Doctor. 'Mankind goes into space to explore. To be part of something greater.'

'But that's all I ever wanted!' Van Statten pleaded. 'I wanted to touch the stars!'

'No,' said the Doctor. 'You just want to drag the stars down, and stick them underground, beneath tons of sand and dirt. And *label* them. You're about as far from the stars as you can get.'

And all of this was true, but still the Doctor saw it on Van Statten's face. *You're the one who killed her. You're the one who let her down.*

And there was nothing to be said about that at all.

Adam heard the laser bolt too. He hadn't moved. He didn't need to move now, did he? He was safe.

The thought popped into his head.

Safe now, it said. *She'll never take away your job now. You're* safe.

Is that what he had wanted? Had there been any part of him that had wanted that? He wasn't sure.

Safe. And the thought made him sick with guilt.

The Genius's Tale

When he was seven, Adam Mitchell decided not to say anything for an entire year.

Later on, psychiatrists would try to get to the bottom of why he'd done that. They'd analyse him from top to toe, and of course by then he was speaking freely, he was happy to tell them anything. Anything they wanted to hear. Some concluded that he'd been very angry. Some that he'd felt alienated from the world. Some that he was simply too intelligent to put up with all the people around him, he'd no longer been able to contribute to their banal conversations when his own thoughts and concerns were on a much higher level, and so he'd had to shut down for a while.

Adam would always agree with whatever conclusions they came up with, and flatter them, and make them feel very clever. On a basic level he was a nice kid, and he wanted everyone to be happy. And maybe there was some truth to what they said. Yes, he had been angry. Yes, he had felt alienated. And yes, he'd become aware that the other children in the playground said such stupid things, and he didn't want to say stupid things, why should he? Adam didn't have many friends. They thought he was odd.

But the truth was, he decided to go silent for a year just to see what would happen.

He didn't tell anyone he was going to do it, of course. That would have ruined the exercise.

He recorded all that happened in a diary he kept hidden under his bed. He liked hiding things there, where only he could find them. It made him feel as if he had secrets.

At first his parents just got very cross. That was predictable enough a response, Adam thought; his parents were often cross with him. They just thought he was being rude. 'You can go to bed without dinner, young man!' And he was willing to oblige.

His teachers thought he was being rude too. And then they changed their minds, they thought he was troubled, and they didn't want anything to do with troubled. So long as he did his homework – and Adam always did his homework very well indeed – they left him alone.

Adam noted how quickly his parents stopped being angry, and started begging him to talk. (Though there was always a bit of anger in their voices, wasn't there? Even when they told him they weren't angry at all.) They promised him anything, everything, so long as he would speak to them. The bribes got bigger and better, from special cakes, to days out at the zoo, to entire holidays. Sometimes they would cry. Adam didn't want to distress them, he wasn't a cruel boy. He tried to show them he was perfectly all right, he'd smile at them a lot. When he wrote them little notes to tell them what he'd like for dinner, he'd draw a happy face at the bottom. Still, they cried anyway.

And sometimes they'd lose their temper, and they'd shout at him, shout right in his face. It just made Adam stick to his guns. If he wasn't going to be coaxed out of his silence with a visit to Alton Towers, he certainly wouldn't give in because they'd threatened to smack him.

What Adam found most interesting was that he didn't *need* to speak. Most basic human needs could be made clear with a nod of the head or a shrug. And now he didn't have to waste time on talking, he realised he could spend it far more profitably inside his own head. His thoughts were wise and quite loquacious, his imaginary vocabulary profound.

He enjoyed the vast open space of his brain.

In time he put away his diary, and he began to write other things, more important things. Sometimes they were stories of aliens. Sometimes they weren't really stories at all, and he knew that he was the alien. Like the diary, he kept them hidden under his bed.

He was taken for tests. Physical tests, mental tests. They discovered he had an IQ that was off the scale. He was quite proud when they told him. He was angry too, it was as if they'd uncovered one of his secrets. He wanted to tell them, I'm only pretending to be a genius! This is just a game! But he mustn't speak, he knew he mustn't, it would spoil everything, and then what would all of this have been for?

What he hadn't expected was how quickly his parents adjusted. They stopped being cross, they stopped begging. They accepted their son wasn't going to speak to them ever again. Christmas Day was hard because they'd put so much effort into it, and he'd been given so many presents, and he'd have liked to thank them. By his birthday in the spring it was much easier, because they hadn't put in the same effort at all.

He didn't cheat. He didn't even talk to himself. He began to wonder over the year whether his tongue had atrophied. He wondered whether, if he ever spoke again, he'd forget what his voice had sounded like and have to invent an entirely new one.

Some time when Adam was eight, he decided to put the silence behind him. A year to the day, and the experiment was over. He felt nervous. He did consider keeping the silence going for another year, just to see what would happen – but he gravely concluded that it was unlikely to produce any fresh results. He allowed himself to feel a certain pride, that he'd lasted the course, that he had set his mind to do something and had had the strength and the commitment to see it through.

He put away his diary and his storybook; he wouldn't need them any longer. He could be ordinary again now, what fun! And then he went downstairs to tell his parents the good news.

Adam had never flown in a helicopter before, but some instinct told him not to look too excited. So he tried to peer incuriously out of the window as they sped ever deeper into the Utah desert, giving every impression that for a 19-year-old boy from Milton Keynes such stuff was something he could take in his stride. The pilot didn't appear to be watching him. Nor did the guard; Adam noticed that the guard had a gun, and he tried not to look excited about that either.

From the helipad he was escorted down one level below the surface. There he was taken to a room, and told to make himself comfortable. There wasn't much within the room to help him with that particular endeavour – a plastic chair, a table with a jug of water upon it – but Adam did his best to comply.

Presently a stern-looking woman entered and said her name was Diana Goddard, and that she would be taking charge of him. Had his flight from London been acceptable? Did he need anything to eat? All these questions, apparently so solicitous for his well-being, asked with cold disregard for whatever his answers might be. Adam began to feel very nervous, and hoped that it wasn't obvious. 'Are you going to interview me for the job now?'

Goddard said, 'That was the interview.'

She told him that Mr Van Statten had been very impressed by the IQ tests Adam had taken when he was a child, and had been watching his subsequent development with great interest. 'Thank you,' said Adam. He wished Goddard herself sounded either impressed or interested. Goddard paused at his interruption, testily waited to see whether Adam had anything further to add; when he didn't, she resumed. Some might have thought to have changed courses at university no fewer than 12 times to be fickle, but Mr Van Statten found it amusing. 'It all just got too easy, I was bored,' said Adam. Goddard paused again, clicked her tongue irritably – she really didn't like being interrupted! – and Adam shut up. And at last she explained to him what his job would entail.

'You shall curate and catalogue Mr Van Statten's collection. We're placing you in sole charge of the inanimates.'

Adam said, 'So there are also animates?'

Goddard wouldn't answer that. But she seemed to soften a little, she sighed. 'May I give you some advice? Mr Van Statten would like to know the origin and function of every little piece of alien trash we buy at auction. But he likes the explanations to be *creative*. We've had experts before who were very good at telling the truth, and the truth was a bit too dull.'

'You want me to lie?'

'Me? I don't want you to do anything!' said Goddard. 'But it would be nice if I stopped having to recruit alien experts every couple of weeks. I have better things to do with my time.'

She took him to his bedroom. It was a small, windowless room with a bunk bed inside. A young man was waiting there for him; only a couple of years older than Adam, he had tried to grow a stubby little beard with inconclusive results.

'This is Sven,' Goddard said. 'You'll be sharing with him. Mr Van Statten says, if you work hard, and he likes what you do, then soon you can have a room to yourself.'

'Oh,' said Adam. 'All right.'

'I should add,' Goddard went on, 'that Sven is *also* in sole charge of the inanimates.' Then she left.

Adam put on a smile he didn't feel, went up to his new roommate, offered him his hand. 'I'm pleased to meet you,' said Adam. 'I look forward to working together.'

Sven looked at Adam's hand as though it were a dead fish, then up at Adam's face. 'I take the top bunk,' he said. 'Try not to get in my way.'

*

Adam hated sharing a room with Sven. In fact, Adam hated Sven. If Adam made any noise, even so much as a single cough, Sven would stop whatever he was doing, turn about, and put an admonishing finger to his lips. Whereas Sven would lie in his precious upper bunk, and snore, and mumble, and fart.

They both worked side by side in the workshop. Sven kept it scrupulously tidy; Adam had to resist the impulse to mess it all up. They'd pore through crates that Mr Van Statten had bought as job lots – metal bits, strange-looking screws and springs, tiny plastic parts that may have been bizarre alien circuitry acting as gateways to brand new technological innovations but may also have been, just as easily, not. Sven would take out an object, turn it over and over in his hands, stare at it unhappily. Then he would scribble down his findings on a piece of card, shielding his work with his hand so Adam couldn't copy. Then Adam would take the same object; he'd examine it from all angles; he'd try to imagine the hundreds and thousands and millions of miles it may have travelled just to finish up on Earth and in his hands. And he'd use that awe to inspire him, and hope that his own explanation was more entertaining than Sven's.

Sometimes it was hard to sleep, especially with all the sounds and smells coming down from the top bunk. Once he'd manage to nod off, Adam would hold tightly to his dreams, and he wouldn't be easily roused in the morning.

One time he was shaken awake, and he opened his eyes reluctantly – only to find it was dark, and Sven was still snoring above him – and two figures were standing over him. He couldn't see their faces. And before he could call out they had put a gag in his mouth; they hauled him from his bunk; they put a bag over his head.

Adam was dragged down a corridor and into a small room. It was only when the ground lurched beneath him that he realised it must be an elevator. The elevator was going down a very long way.

At last the descent was over. Adam had no idea how deep he'd be taken, but he swallowed hard to try to make his ears pop. The bag was pulled off his head, and Adam found himself looking into the face of a man whose smile showed too many teeth.

'Now,' said the toothy-smiled man. 'What's your name?'

Adam didn't want to tell this man anything. But he told him anyway.

'Well, Adam,' grinned the man, 'I gather you're in charge of the inanimates! So I thought we should meet. I'm Simmons, and I deal with the living stuff. We're colleagues! It's a real pleasure to meet you.' And Simmons gave Adam his hand, and Adam took it, and Simmons squeezed it, and it hurt.

'What do you want from me?' asked Adam, as bravely as he could.

Simmons looked pained. 'Now, don't be like that! It's just a bit of fun! We do it to all the newbies, right, fellers?' The two guards who had brought Adam down grunted non-committally. 'You up there, near the sunlight, scratching away at pieces of crap. I thought you'd like to meet a proper alien.'

In spite of himself Adam said, 'You've got something alive down here?'

'Sure,' said Simmons. 'Want to take a look?' And then all Adam knew was that he was shoved into a dark room, and a heavy door was slammed behind him.

Adam heard Simmons over a speaker. 'Seeing as you're an expert, I thought you might be able to help with a little problem I'm having.'

'It's too dark,' said Adam. 'I can't see. Is there an alien in here? I can't see!'

'Patience,' said Simmons. 'The creature is resting. I'm turning the light up by degrees, we don't want to shock it. Can you see it yet?'

Adam could.

'All I'm trying to do,' said Simmons, 'is get it to talk. Any bright ideas? Why not get closer?' And the voice hardened. 'But don't touch.'

Adam forgot to be frightened. He stepped forward. All those bits of metal he had to find excitement for in the workshop – and here was something *real*, something that had lived beyond the stars.

'You can't force it to talk,' said Adam.

'Why not? What do you know about it?'

'It'll talk when it's ready,' said Adam. 'It's waiting.'

'Waiting for what?' But Adam wasn't listening to Simmons any longer – he was staring hard at the alien that, like him, had decided to play silent. 'Hey,' he whispered to it, 'it's all right. You take your time.'

And at that, the thing that looked like an eyestalk jerked into life and swung towards him, and Adam recoiled – he just couldn't help it.

'Time to come out,' said Simmons.

Then Adam saw that one of the creature's arms was pointing at him. The one a bit like an egg whisk, flexing over and over again with increasing urgency.

Simmons was behind him now. 'That's enough,' he said.

'Look,' said Adam. 'Maybe it's speaking to us this very moment. That little cylinder on the side, maybe that's the tongue.'

Simmons looked puzzled. 'Then why can't we hear anything?'

'Maybe,' said Adam, 'I don't know, maybe it's on a different frequency. Like a dog whistle. I bet that's it! It's chatting away to us, but it's outside the range of human hearing.'

'That won't please Mr Van Statten,' said Simmons. 'So you better not be right.'

Outside the Cage, the guards had a tot of whisky to drink. He had passed the initiation test! He said he didn't want it. They made him drink it anyway.

'You got a name for it?' asked Simmons. 'Mr Van Statten wants a new one. We've been calling it Pepperpotnik, but he's got fed up with it.'

'It's sort of metal,' said Adam. 'A Metaltron?'

Simmons looked as if he would laugh in Adam's face. Then said, 'I'll give it a try.' He bent towards Adam, spoke to him confidentially, even kindly. 'You know,' he said, 'I could really hurt you if I wanted to.'

'I bet you could,' said Adam.

'You'd be right.'

'OK.'

'You did better than most. Sometimes they get really scared.' And he looked so disappointed, and when he took Adam's hand in farewell he crushed it even harder than before.

Adam went back upstairs to his room. Sven was snoring, but it sounded fake. 'Did you know that was going to happen?' shouted Adam. 'Is that what they did to you?'

Adam thought Sven wasn't even going to reply. Then Sven said softly, 'Just get to sleep.'

And since there was nothing else for it, that's what Adam did.

Adam never expected to meet Henry Van Statten. But then, one day, he was summoned.

Van Statten was all smiles; Goddard, standing by his side, had none. 'It is so good to meet you at last!' said his boss, and he actually rose from his chair to greet him. 'You've been doing excellent work with my collection.' He was as warm and charming and kind as the huge portrait behind his desk seemed to indicate; Adam immediately knew he was terrified of him.

'Thank you, sir,' said Adam.

'Oh, and he's English!' Van Statten looked at Goddard. ' Got to love the English, the way they talk. How long did our last English one last? ... Oh, it doesn't matter! And I love your accounts of my artefacts, they're so inventive!'

'Thank you, sir,' said Adam again.

'But you don't want to get too inventive,' said Van Statten. 'It's a fine line. You don't want to think me an idiot.'

'No.'

'No!' All smiles again. 'Good boy. So, are you happy here? The work, the food, the accommodation? Oh, speaking about that. Goddard tells me you're having to share a room. Well, we can put that right in an instant. How would you like a room of your own?'

'Thank you, sir,' said Adam. 'Yes, that would make everything much better.'

'Be sure, Adam Mitchell from England,' said Van Statten. 'Everything has consequences.'

Adam frowned. He looked to Goddard for help, but she studiously managed to avoid eye contact. She looked furious. *Don't involve me in any of this*, her face seemed to say. *Keep me out of it.*

'Yes, please,' Adam said quietly.

'What was that? Speak up.'

'Yes. I would like my own room.'

'Good. Bring him in, then,' said Van Statten.

Two guards appeared, each holding Sven by one arm.

'Please!' cried Sven. 'I won't say anything!' In all the weeks Adam had spent with his roommate, the boy had never done more than mutter at him. It was a genuine shock to realise Sven could raise his voice.

'Of course you won't,' said Van Statten smoothly. 'Sit him down, boys.' He put on a single black glove, then pulled out from a desk drawer a small metal orb. It seemed to sparkle in the light.

'This is a useful device we recovered from the Tunguska meteor impact,' said Van Statten. 'Our own version of the non-disclosure agreement.' And almost delicately he pressed the ball against Sven's head.

At once Sven stiffened. As if every muscle in his face had become tight, Adam could see them all bulging against the skin. Even his pathetic scrap of a beard went rigid, all the fur stuck out pointed and sharp, and it acquired a grandeur that heretofore had been sadly lacking.

'All the memories of Sven's time here belong to me under contract, and will be extracted,' said Van Statten. 'Clean and painless.'

'Painless?'

'So I imagine.'

From out of the orb snaked a thin metal finger. It wrapped itself around Sven's face. If Sven was in pain, he'd forgotten how to show it. Already his face had slumped, his eyes rolling back into the skull. And the metal finger seemed to thicken as it pumped faster, as it drank deep.

'That's extraordinary,' Adam made himself say. 'So how does it know to wipe only the memories you want it to?'

'You know,' said Van Statten, 'it would be just great to work that out.'

The finger was fat and bloated. It peeled itself off Sven's face with a wet sucking sound, and then snapped itself back inside the orb.

The boy looked around the room dazedly, He opened his mouth to speak, and then, slowly, closed it again. He started to drool.

'Thanks for your service, Sven from Norway,' said Van Statten. 'We'll get you safely home.'

'I think,' said Goddard quietly, 'he's from Sweden.'

'We'll drop him off somewhere in Scandinavia, that's close enough.' Van Statten waved his hand, and the guards helped Sven to his feet. As he was bundled out of the door, Sven seemed to recognise Adam. His face lit up, and he smiled at him.

Adam looked at Goddard, and her face was so impassive, she didn't dare to react. And Adam made his face impassive too, he stared down at the floor.

'There you are, English kid. One room, all to yourself,' Van Statten said. 'We only want you to be comfortable. We're very pleased with your progress, so far. And I am sure I shall be seeing a lot more of you.'

By the time Adam had got back to his quarters all traces of Sven had been removed. Everything gone – even the smell.

Later that day Adam went to the workshop, and he began opening up all the crates, and tipping the contents out on to the floor. And any time he saw anything that even resembled a weapon he smuggled it back to his room, and hid it under the bed. He liked keeping things under the bed. It made him feel as if he had secrets.

Oddly enough, even though Sven was gone, Adam didn't sleep any better.

9

Rose Tyler was alive. She didn't know why. She had felt the heat of the laser bolt as the Dalek had fired upon her – she could still feel it now, tingling against her skin. She could smell it. And yet she was unharmed.

It couldn't have simply missed her. Not at point-blank range. She watched as the Dalek aimed its gunstick once more, prepared to fire. Hesitated.

'Get on with it!' she shouted. Because the anticipation was so cruel, it was worse than actual death, wasn't it? Wasn't it?

And still the Dalek didn't shoot. It stared straight at her. Probing her mind, it was so close, and so *big*, like a huge fist inside her head squeezing at her thoughts.

The quiet was unendurable. Only seconds of life left, each moment wondering whether this breath was to be her last – or this one, or this one ... She shouted because she had to fill the quiet, she refused to die in silence.

'Why are you doing this? You've killed all those people ...!'

'I gave myself orders,' the Dalek told her.

'And did you *enjoy them*?'

'My function is to kill. Why else would I be armed?'

'They're all dead because of you!'

'No,' the Dalek said. 'They are dead because of *us*.'

The simple truth of it was awful. And that's when Rose gave up. She couldn't shout any more.

'So now what?' she said. 'What are you waiting for?'

The Dalek stumbled over its words. 'I feel … I can feel your fear.'

'What do you expect?'

'But Daleks do not fear! It is not permitted!' Rose heard the rising panic in its voice – this was not merely fear, the creature was terrified. 'Daleks *must* not fear!'

And it fired its gun at her, twice. The first shot struck the wall just above her shoulder. The second singed her hair. And still it could not kill her.

'I can feel your fear, Rose Tyler, deep inside me! You gave me life! What else have you given me?'

Adam Mitchell had at last made it upstairs to Van Statten's office. And the Doctor had wanted to rage at him, how *dare* he be the one who survived? How could he have made it through, when Rose Tyler was dead? It wasn't fair. But he didn't. He wouldn't. Not because he was being kind, but because he knew that once he let his fury out he'd never be able to rein it back in, and it would be over. He didn't know what he would become.

Adam sat in a corner of the room, and didn't say anything, and looked guilty. *Good*, thought the Doctor. *I hope your guilt chokes you.*

He would save his rage for the Dalek. Because he knew he hadn't seen the last of it. Sooner or later it would reappear on the screen, and demand to be released from the vaults. Would it beg? The Doctor hoped it would beg.

And of course, it did appear. And of course, it didn't beg.

'I have restored the power to the bulkhead. Open it, or Rose Tyler dies.'

It was true, Rose was standing next to it, Rose was alive. The Doctor felt such a sudden rush of relief – and then sick, because he knew now what would happen. He'd have to sacrifice her all over again. Kill her all over again. And this time, the Dalek would force him to watch. And he *would* watch, too – he wouldn't be able to look away.

'Rose,' he called out, uselessly. He couldn't stop himself.

'Open the bulkhead door at once!' the Dalek insisted.

'Don't do it!' It was Rose. 'He's bluffing, he can't kill me …!'

The Doctor thought, *He?*

And the sucker arm shot out, it slapped itself hard over Rose's mouth. 'Do not dare presume,' hissed the Dalek, 'to tell me what I can or cannot do.' Its eyestalk returned to the camera, it gazed at the Doctor defiantly.

The Doctor gazed back, the agony of indecision.

The Dalek said, 'You are a creature of emotion, Doctor. But what use are emotions if you will not save the woman you love?'

'What do you know of love?' The Doctor was yelling – and was this it? Was this the moment he let the fury out, and lost himself forever? 'When the hell has a Dalek ever used the word "love"?'

The Dalek just watched him.

'Doctor?' Goddard said.

'Please?' said Van Statten.

Kill her again.

'No,' said the Doctor.

And he tapped at the keyboard, and the bulkhead door began to rise. He wondered if that was when the Dalek would kill Rose anyway, one last moment of cruelty, to show him he'd saved her for nothing. He waited for it. He deserved it. But then the video screen went blank.

'What do we do now?' moaned Van Statten. There was no anger left in him, and no pride. The Doctor looked at him dully, and realised the man was in tears.

Adam said, 'Why don't we just kill it when it gets here?'

Van Statten was so surprised by the boy's idiocy he forgot to cry.

Goddard snapped, 'All our guns are useless, and the alien weapons are in the vaults!'

'Only the catalogued ones,' said Adam, a little sulkily. And that's when he told them about everything he kept hidden under his bed.

It was as if the Doctor had been in a deep pit, and he couldn't talk or reason – it was over, everything was finally done. And somehow, without even trying, he'd broken to the surface.

There was hope after all. It was almost easier when there hadn't been.

'Show me,' he told Adam. 'Now.'

The Dalek released Rose Tyler from its grasp, and Rose Tyler recoiled from it angrily, and that was to be expected – but then why did the Dalek feel ashamed? What could that mean?

'I saw the love in your thoughts,' the Dalek said 'That *need*.'

'You can't tell me that *you* don't need,' said Rose Tyler.

The Dalek thought about this. 'The Doctor. Would you die for him?'

'I don't know.'

'You do know. I have seen the answer. You would die.'

'Then why ask me?'

'There are also things I would die for,' said the Dalek. 'We are not so different, you and I.'

There was a little boy standing on a hill.

The Dalek and Rose Tyler approached the elevator to the upper levels. The Dalek restored its power.

The Dalek said, 'I was bred to kill, and then to die. And I was not afraid. Death was part of my function. But you revived me. By giving me life, you gave me choice.'

'Yes,' said Rose.

'I was never intended to have choice.'

'Please,' said Rose Tyler, and the Dalek did not want to listen, but it had to listen. 'You don't have to kill any more. You didn't kill me. You can be better than this.' It had to listen, but it would rather have Rose Tyler's voice out of its mind, it would rather she were dead.

It wanted to scream at her to be silent, or it would exterminate her. It couldn't.

The little boy stood on a hill, and he was flying a kite.

'There are nothing but choices,' whispered the Dalek. 'I see that now. How can you endure it?'

The lift arrived. The door opened.

'There is a world inside you,' said the Dalek. 'I thought you were small. You are not small. All of your thoughts. Beliefs. Ideas. How do you not drown in them? Who are you, Rose Tyler? Who is the Bad Wolf?'

The little boy stood on a hill, flying his kite. And the sky was so heavy, and he couldn't hold it back any longer.

'Do not leave me, Rose Tyler,' said the Dalek.

Rose Tyler said, 'I won't.'

They got into the lift.

The Soldier's Tale

The little boy stood on a hill. But it wasn't a hill any longer, was it? – it was being crushed flat. The sky was falling, and who could have guessed the sky was so heavy? It bore down upon the little boy's head, and it was so vast and so fierce and so unyielding and the boy thought he would burst open under the pressure. The sky was like a finger, and it was pressing the boy down ever deeper into the hill, and the hill was fast disappearing, it would soon be lost, and then the boy would be lost, and there would be nothing left. Nothing.

And for the first time in his life, the little boy knew terror.

He began to scream, and his mouth opened wide to let the terror out, and it was as wide as the sky, and into his stupid gaping mouth the sky flooded in.

He heard the voice speak in his head. *Observe your fear. You will never feel fear again. Fear is what we shall inflict upon* them.

In his last surviving seconds, he heard that same voice add: *From now, all fear is forbidden.*

The little boy supposed that should have been reassuring, but it very really wasn't.

A full seven seconds after he had been born, the child was taken from the nursery, and plugged into the emotional centres of the memory grid. It might have been sooner, but High Command had designated a seven-second delay, the length of time most optimally suited to instil the correct level of disorientation. It made the infants more vulnerable, and therefore more readily able to understand their function. Besides, it was hard to get them there any faster, there were a lot of children to process.

Sometimes the memory grid would show a woman in a garden, or a man boating on a lake. A little girl playing on the swings, all alone, and on every upward arc the swing would take her higher into the air and she'd whoop with joy. A boy standing on a hill flying a kite.

It didn't matter which unreality the children were presented with. The individual experiences were never the point. So long as for just the shortest while in their mean existence they could taste joy, and freedom, and peace. So long as they could feel the sunlight.

All extracted from the dying dreams of their enemies. Final fantasies of happiness, just before their lives had been snuffed out.

Remember that joy, the children were told.

Remember, and resent it. Remember what other life forms take for granted. That which will be denied you forever. Remember what they have and you do not, these creatures that are no better than you are, no more worthy of happiness than you.

For you shall never feel peace. Or a cooling breeze, or the sunlight on your skin.

For you shall never feel desire, unless it is the communal desire to better our superior race.

For you shall never again be on your own.

The child thought back to the little boy on the hill, the little boy that had been so happy and had then been so afraid. The little boy that had been him. And he hated him, and he wanted to kill him, he wanted to exterminate him over and over without end and without mercy.

The child had had his Grand Revelation, and everyone seemed pleased with him. He now knew that happiness in life was a delusion too soon snatched away. And all the beings who laboured under that delusion were inferior, and needed to be corrected by force.

As a reward, he was taken to his new home. Home was a casing of battle armour, and how shiny it looked, and it was all for him! He couldn't quite fit within the interior cavity. He was assured that was perfectly normal, all the children mutated differently, and no one ever was quite the right size or shape. Why, some were born like squids, some like spiders, some like creatures so grotesquely malformed it would seem heresy to give them a name at all. It was not a problem. There was a procedure for just this eventuality. And they took hold of all his extraneous limbs, and they hacked them off. And then they assessed which body parts were still jutting out and preventing the casing from shutting neatly, and they hacked them off too. For some reason the child had been born with two good eyes when only one was deemed necessary, so they put the other out with a spike.

The child was then reassured that all the surplus would not go to waste. It would be taken to the incubation vats, and there would provide tissue necessary for the creation of more children. And he wanted to cry out with jubilation, because he had already been of service to the empire. He could not do so, though, as his vocal cords were in the process of being severed, to make way for more reliable metal-synth replacements.

They fixed his flesh into final position with bolts and screws, and that was agony, and the agony was never going to go away. But it was good, because the child had a second Grand Revelation. That agony in life was more reliable and more constant than hope of happiness could ever be.

They told him finally that his mutations were individual, and therefore shameful. But now he would be absolved of sin. His individuality would be shut away within his metal shell and never again be seen. And they closed the casing upon him, and his world got so much smaller and so much tighter – so tight that the child thought he wouldn't be able to breathe! But he needn't have been concerned, there was a tube inserted sharp into his lungs to take care of breaths for him. He looked out of his eyestalk and saw that they had been right – he was surrounded on all sides by lots of other children, his fellows in the great wars ahead, and he couldn't tell a single one apart.

All the children were taken for classification. They were loaded onto conveyor belts and scanned. An operator would judge them, one by one. 'Soldier,' it would say; another child would roll up. 'Soldier. Soldier. Soldier.'

He could have been designated a Commander – that was one child in a hundred thousand. He could have been a Supreme – that was one in a billion. But he was just a soldier. Of course he was a soldier. That was right.

His function would always be to follow orders, and never to give them. The child relaxed in his casing. That would make his life much less complicated.

The child was a soldier, and now it had to think of itself as a soldier. But sometimes it would still remember it was a child. It tried not to, but it was there, right at the very core of his being. He thought of the little boy on the hill. The little boy disgusted him. And that child part of himself, that tiny scrap of innocence he couldn't get rid of, that disgusted him too.

The soldier was put into a training squad, and assigned a Commander.

The Commander said, 'This is your purpose. You work to ensure the continued survival of our race. Nothing else matters. Together we are the most powerful beings the universe has ever known. Alone, we are nothing.'

The soldier fixed upon the Commander with his one remaining eye, and it committed the image to his memory banks. 'Commander,' he said to himself, designating the image a definition. 'Father,' he added, quietly.

Only days later the Commander was killed in an attack upon the Kasterborous constellation. It was a great victory, and ensured the continued dominance of the race, and it was right that the Commander had died. The soldier did not know whether the Commander had fought bravely, or died for a particular reason, because no one told him. And yet he *did* know, of course he knew – the Commander had fought bravely, the Commander had died for a reason.

The soldier was assigned a new Commander. He looked the same. He sounded the same. He was different. The Commander gave the squad its instructions.

'This is your purpose. Together we are invincible. Alone, nothing.' And the soldier committed the new Commander to memory, and erased all trace of the old one. 'Commander,' he said. 'Father.'

The soldier went to war, as all soldiers have to do. He was told that his people had been fighting wars for countless millennia. And all the wars had been significant, but this particular war was the most significant war yet. And this was the war he would die in.

He should feel proud to be a part of the greatest moment of history. He was proud.

The Commander addressed the squad. They were to launch an attack on Arcadia, a city on their hated enemy's home planet. The soldier didn't know whether this was the same Commander who had spoken to them all yesterday; the constant erasure and update of his memory banks had him confused. 'We shall conquer Arcadia, and raze it to the ground. It will be a great victory. You have all been designated to be amongst the first casualties.'

The soldier felt pleased, because at last he knew he had a destiny, and really, it was such a very simple one.

The Commander went on, and there was a slight raise of pitch in his voice, it became shrill with urgency. 'Our greatest foe will be at the battle. He is called the Doctor, a man of ever-changing faces. Every soldier you meet may be the Doctor. Fear the Doctor! Exterminate him! Fear the Doctor! Exterminate him!'

The squad took up the chant, and the soldier chanted alongside them. And he thought, but hadn't fear been forbidden? Hadn't he been given the promise he would never feel fear again? But he knew he must have misunderstood somehow, and kept quiet.

The soldier saw the Commander die, blasted apart by a staser bolt. But in the retaliatory fire three of the enemy were exterminated, so that was good, the Commander had died a useful death. The soldier briefly wondered who his next Commander would be, and then remembered that he would be dead very soon himself, and so the matter was irrelevant.

He wondered what death would be like. Whether it would be painful. Whether it would be immediate, so he wouldn't even notice. He hoped he would notice, that he'd live long enough to experience something. Painful would feel less like a cheat.

But he didn't hope too much. It was just a vague and dispassionate thing; he knew, really, that his death had very little to do with him.

Yet he did not die.

All around him on the battlefield there was carnage. Bodies broken in the dirt, or crushed under rubble, or split open by enemy fire – he could see the children in death, all those hidden mutations at last peeping through.

But he did not die. He did not avoid it. It seemed to avoid him.

And then for a while the soldier was all alone, and he fought down a rising panic, because he was never supposed to be alone, he had been assured he would never be alone. But he couldn't see anyone – not a single living being – not through the clouds of ash and smoke. Could he be the last survivor? Were the enemy all dead, and were his comrades all dead?

Was he the only one left alive at the end of the greatest war in history?

Was the final victory his and only his and no one else's, no one else's in the whole universe? And if so, what was he to do with that victory? What would be the point? What was his purpose?

He picked his way across the rubble for eternal minutes, and he thought he could now hear the sound of distant gunfire, but could no longer be sure it wasn't a fantastical memory. The little boy stood on a hill. The little boy stood in the ruins of a fallen world. The child began to feel afraid. The child wanted to howl.

Suddenly he saw a figure, coming through the smoke, its features silhouetted against the fire. An enemy soldier, but that did not matter – it was life – and the soldier felt a surge of relief.

The man saw him at the same time.

They both fell still.

The man was elderly, white hair on his face, and even through the thick fog the soldier could see how his eyes burned with age and with fury.

He was not carrying a weapon.

Of all the men the soldier had seen and killed, this one alone was unarmed – and he was staring straight at the soldier with undisguised contempt, and he was not afraid.

The soldier knew who the man had to be.

The soldier raised his gunstick.

The soldier knew he had to kill him, but he felt fear, he felt so much fear.

And they stood like that, the Dalek and the Doctor. Facing each other down on the final battlefield. They stood like that forever. For a few seconds.

Then the Doctor turned away. He just turned away, he didn't dignify the soldier with with so much as another glance. He walked into the fog, and was lost.

The soldier fired his gun at last. But he was not firing at the Doctor. He was firing into the chaos, pointless laser bolts that would never find a target. He fired his gun over and over, until the effort of firing began to hurt. *He began to hurt.*

And then onwards through the darkness, trying to find the Doctor, trying to hide from the Doctor, trying to kill the Doctor, trying to be killed.

The little boy.

On and on, over the wreckage, until the ground gave way, and at last the soldier fell.

Is this death? he thought. *Or some kind of death? Or at least, some kind of extinction of which I need not feel ashamed?*

The little boy stood on a hill, until the hill was crushed beneath him.

The soldier fell, and he fell for a very long time, longer than should ever have been possible.

The soldier thought he might break on impact, but he was not that lucky – it was the ground that broke, and down he went into the earth. And inside the crater he burned inside his casing for three days, and he screamed. In pain, in fear, in humiliation? The soldier no longer even knew. And still he could not die.

The enemy came for him, and he was outraged that they trapped him in a cell and did not put him to death.

They tortured him. The soldier did not know why. They told him to speak. The soldier knew he had no words of any value. Even so, because they wanted his words so badly, he refused to give them any.

One day they brought him the Doctor, and the soldier was excited, and he gripped on so tightly to the Doctor's hand and would not let him go. But it was not the Doctor, it was a fake Doctor, and the man burst into flames. The soldier felt this encounter was a tactical error. He had been still and quiet for years, and only now had broken cover. But it felt good to watch the man burn.

Sometimes as they tortured him bits of his body would spill out through the cracks in his casing and leak on to the floor. The soldier made himself believe that none of those bits were essential to his function.

It would have been so easy just to have died. But he had no such instructions.

A voice in the darkness. A new voice. It doesn't demand. It doesn't beg. 'I'm here to help. I'm the Doctor.'

Another trick? The soldier will not be deceived again. And the man that stands before him does not resemble the grizzled warrior he met on the battlefield. But his eyes. His eyes still burn like before.

The soldier tries to kill him. This time he will not fail. He raises his gun, and pumps laser bolts at his enemy. Exterminate. Exterminate. Exterminate.

The Doctor doesn't die. He laughs.

Once again, the soldier cannot kill him. But at least this time the failure is not a matter of nerve. The gun is no longer functional.

And still the Doctor is laughing, and now sneering, and now raging. The soldier is powerless against his contempt. He wants to escape. He cannot escape.

Then in an instant the soldier reaches three conclusions. And if they are contradictory, it doesn't matter. Because each of them is pure.

The soldier thinks, I shall kill the Doctor. Or he shall kill me. And either way there shall be an end.

The soldier thinks, the Doctor is the only survivor of the war. He's the only one fit to command me. He shall give me orders.

The soldier thinks – no, the *child* thinks –

The child thinks, *Father.*

10

Henry Van Statten remembered the day he'd acquired the Dalek as one of the proudest of his life. The large wooden crate was set upon the desert floor, just above the lift hatch that would take it down into his museum forever – and Henry could barely wait, he was like a small child on Christmas Day, he wanted to tear the box open with his bare hands so he could get to see his pet. He knew the creature would be fragile, it could only be released in laboratory conditions, and there was a storm coming, the sand was starting to whip around his face and neck. But it hurt him that he still had to wait, he had already waited so long, and there were still more minutes to go before he could have what he wanted. It was a good hurt. It excited him. And he pressed his ear to the side of the crate. He couldn't hear anything. He knew he was close to it. Close at long last.

In the laboratory it was revealed that the creature was not in mint condition. There were dents all over the body. Its base was warped, so it didn't so much stand as loll. It looked shabby. It looked dirty. And it was a pepperpot, of all things – with two ridiculous arms. For a moment Van Statten couldn't decide whether he would express disappointment or not. To love it, or to hate it. The technicians all about him held their breaths, waiting for his verdict. 'Doesn't look all that impressive, does it?' one of them dared to say, and immediately Van Statten had him both dismissed and mind-wiped. No, he was going to love it. He wouldn't give up on it. It showed promise.

He had visited it so often in its cell, sometimes he would spend entire days down there just staring at it, and looking over every inch of its body. Knowing the placement of every crack and scratch – getting to know the placement of new ones he had his technicians create.

And now it was in his office, standing right before him – and it was as if Van Statten saw it properly for the first time. Fully healed, its battle armour savage and gold gleaming. Strong, remorseless. And he felt a thrill of pride – just look at it! He was right to place such faith in it. It was like a child who had matured and at last proved its potential.

His silly little broken toy, how beautiful it had become. He loved it. And it terrified him.

He proudly took it all in. The Dalek twitching as it surveyed the room. It seemed unimpressed by the décor, by the Argentinian portrait staring down at it so condescendingly. The Doctor's friend behind it –

'Don't move!' she said. 'Don't do anything to alarm it!' Goddard taking her gun out – the Dalek swivelling its eyestalk to her – Goddard surrendering, throwing the gun to the floor.

The Dalek seeing him, at last.

'Van Statten,' it said. For so long that was all Henry had wanted, to hear his creature say his name, to acknowledge him. The name was spat out like an insult. 'You tortured me. Why?'

Henry's words poured out in a rush. 'I wanted to help you. I don't know. I just wanted to look after you, you're a survivor, we're both survivors! If you could guess at the things I've had to do ...!' He heard himself saying all this, and it disgusted him, and he could only imagine how it would disgust his Dalek. Where was the Henry Van Statten that could smoothly quell dissent in any boardroom with one raised inflection of the voice? He forced himself to stop babbling. 'I wanted,' he said, more slowly, 'to make you talk.'

The Dalek thought about this. 'What would you have had me say?'

Henry was surprised. That had genuinely never occurred to him. 'I don't know,' he said.

'Very well,' said the Dalek. 'You shall hear me talk. Exterminate! Exterminate! Exterminate!'

The gunstick, taking aim.

Van Statten closed his eyes, knowing he was about to die.

'No!' he heard the English girl cry. He dared look – she was by the Dalek's side, and the Dalek had turned to look at her, it was listening to her so carefully. 'No,' she said again, more gently.

The Dalek hesitated. Then, 'No,' it agreed, and it turned away. It started to leave the room.

Henry Van Statten was dismissed.

It was over. He knew somehow he would never see it again.

This couldn't be how it ended.

He called out, 'I was right to want you, wasn't I? You are magnificent.'

And the Dalek was back, and this time it went right up to Henry's face, he was forced to back hard against the wall. There was nowhere to move, he was inches away from it, and perhaps he shouldn't have said anything, but now this close, closer to the Dalek than he had ever dared, he knew it was true, it was *magnificent*, it was true. 'Touch me,' said the Dalek, quietly.

'I can't,' said Henry. The memory of Dr Kandinsky bursting into flame, the smell of that. 'Please. I'll die.'

'No,' said the Dalek. 'I shall extract nothing from you. There is nothing in you I could want.'

Henry prodded the Dalek with his finger. He didn't die.

He relaxed somewhat, pressed his palm against the casing. As Rose Tyler had done, as Kandinsky had done. It was warm and surprisingly smooth. He felt honoured.

'Thank you,' he said. 'Thank you.' But the Dalek had moved away, and it was really gone now, it was out of the door without deigning to give Henry one last look.

Henry looked down at his hand. Without the warmth of the Dalek's metal skin it felt cold, so very cold.

He closed his eyes.

There was a little boy on a hill.

And he knew the little boy was him. The hill was so tall, and it was night time, wasn't it? All the stars were out. He could even reach them. He knew he could, if he just stretch up as tall as he could go, up on his tippy-toes with his arm out. Let's see him try! Yes, look! He scraped the stars with his fingers. They tingled.

There was a man climbing the hill to join him. He recalled him vaguely – he was carrying a telescope. 'This is for you, Henry, it's all for you!' The German accent – it was Otto, how could he ever have forgotten him? Henry's heart swelled to see his old childhood friend, the one man who had been kind to him and protected him … and then Otto was dead. Otto was dead, he had shot Otto dead.

He hadn't realised he was carrying a gun. And then he understood that he was the gun.

'No!' he cried out, and he wanted to hold Otto in his arms, but his arms didn't quite work that way. 'No!' he cried again, and his voice was wrong, it was harsh and grating.

More people came up the hill. 'I love my job,' said the President, so he shot him. 'I can't produce art that's culturally sterile,' said a famous painter, so he shot him. 'I shan't sell you my monster,' said Hiram Duchesne, so he shot him. 'Doesn't look all that impressive, does it?' said some nameless scientist, and so Henry shot him again and again and again.

And the bodies burned, and he smelled blood, and he heard the screams of the dying. Every single memory he had, collapsing in on themselves and turning to mulch, and in each of them he was killing everyone, because killing was his only function. And with each new murder he felt such hatred and such despair.

There were so many people on the hill now, they blotted out all the stars in the night sky. They blocked the view of the fields and the trees and the lakes. He would destroy every last one of them. 'Father!' he called. 'Father!' His father wouldn't speak to him, so he shot him. There he was again, climbing one of the trees – 'Father!' he screamed, and his father wouldn't look at him, so he shot him. There he was again, bathing in one of the lakes – 'Father, for God's sake, father! Talk to me! You will talk to me!' And his father wouldn't love him, so he shot him.

Everyone on the hill was now Edward Van Statten, and the more of them Henry exterminated the more of them he had to kill.

Henry had no hands, he had a gun and he had a sucker. And yet he could feel his hands as they searched through the drawers to his desk, feverishly trying to identify them by touch. At last they settled upon a metal orb.

He pressed it hard against his head. And for a few seconds nothing happened, and Henry thought even this little alien ball had rejected him too. That it would refuse to feed off memories as poisonous and corrupted as his.

Then, at last, a metal finger snaked out, and wrapped itself around Henry's face. The mind screamed for a moment with awful pain – and then it stopped, it didn't know what pain was any more.

Goddard walked over to Henry Van Statten. He was lying on the floor, and he was dribbling. Staring up at her without recognition, managing a sort of hopeful smile. 'Daddy?'

She could have kicked him. She wanted to kick him. No one would ever have known. Henry Van Statten himself – he would never have known.

She thought about Bywater. 'By any means necessary,' she said. She helped the adult baby to its feet, and set him down in a chair, and tried to wipe away all the drool.

11

The Dalek determined that the outer wall was at its weakest beneath the helipad. One laser bolt fired upwards would breach it satisfactorily.

He told Rose Tyler this, and Rose Tyler smiled, and said, 'So, you've made it! You're free!' And then she frowned, and the Dalek didn't like it when Rose Tyler frowned, all that new confusion in his mind. 'Well, why don't you do it, then? Isn't this what you wanted?'

The Dalek didn't know what he wanted. But Rose's suggestion sounded like an order, or perhaps the closest to an order he was going to get. So he dutifully fired. Rubble rained down – and there was a hole in the roof – and through it a blue cloudless sky, as wide as the Dalek could imagine.

A shaft of light poured in through the hole, and Rose walked into it, and raised her face towards it, and closed her eyes. 'Never thought I'd feel the sunlight again,' she said.

'How does it feel?' the Dalek asked.

The Dalek had been sealed within his casing as a newborn child, and had never known whether it could be opened. The notion, simply, had never occurred to him. Even the idea of such freedom was heretical. But the idea was in his head now. Oh, he had so many ideas.

With a simple thought, pushed by his brain in the right direction and with just the right force, the Dalek could hear the whirrs and creaks as his own shell split open and let the light in.

Rose could at last see what he really looked like. For the first time, the Dalek realised, she truly knew him. He could feel her revulsion. That the sight of him truly sickened her, in spite of herself.

But then, something stronger – a growing resolve not to be frightened, or disgusted, or cruel. A sympathy. Even an understanding.

Released from the constraints of its metal jail, the Dalek could feel his body ooze out of place. Some of him dripped out of the casing altogether. The Dalek chose not to care.

He reached a single tendril out towards the sunlight. The tendril was nothing but a series of nerve endings, and for countless years all of them had been hot with pain. Now there was a different warmth – a soothing warmth. The Dalek basked in it.

Rose had felt revolted, it was true. That slab of flesh, reddened by sores where it had been pierced by ugly bolts of metal. And she could see where there might once have been a head, and a stomach, and limbs – but over time, and without the space to grow, they had all blurred into one, a hideous mass of body forced to close in on itself to survive. What she made herself look at was the eye. Just one single eye, peering out from the obscene prison of skin and sinew holding it in place. It was the one body part she could properly identify. It was the one thing that revealed to her the creature this should have been. The eye looked old and sad and unspeakably tired.

Behind her she heard a voice. 'Rose! Get out of the way!'

It was the Doctor. But for a moment she couldn't recognise him. It wasn't just because he was carrying a huge gun, and was aiming it directly at her. It was the cold determination on his face. She could have taken anger, she would have been all right with that. But not the coldness.

'No,' she said.

And a flutter of something else that was new across the Doctor's face. Surprise? No, more – shock.

'I'm not going to let you do this,' she said.

'That thing killed hundreds of people. I've got to do this. Got to end it. The Daleks destroyed my people, I've got nothing left.'

'There's not a single Dalek that should be saved? Not one you can forgive?'

'No,' said the Doctor. 'They're all the same. They're all exactly the same.'

'It's not the one pointing the gun at me.'

The Doctor looked as if he had been slapped.

'Look at it,' Rose said. 'Just *look at it.*'

So the Doctor looked. He stared at it in new bewilderment.

'It couldn't kill Van Statten,' said Rose. 'It couldn't kill me. It's changing. And what about you, Doctor? What the hell are you changing into?'

The Doctor said, 'I couldn't ...'

He tried again. 'I wasn't ...'

The Doctor, wrestling with his words. The man who was never lost for something to say. With whom she'd faced down death, and won through against unbeatable odds – and Rose had known that their luck would run out sooner or later and the odds would be just too great, but she never doubted that up until the end he'd be by her side, being brave and making jokes and *talking*. And his mouth was wide open, but there were no words coming out – it was like a silent howl. 'Oh, Rose,' he managed, his voice so soft. 'They're all dead. My people. They're all dead.'

And it was the Dalek who answered him.

'Why do we survive?'

'Why do we survive?' It wasn't a taunt, the Dalek's question was sincere. It was recognising the same struggle, and responding to it. Trying against hope to understand.

'I don't know,' said the Doctor.

'I want to kill you,' said the Dalek. 'I think … I think it may be the only thing I have ever wanted for myself.'

'I understand.'

'I cannot kill you.'

'No,' said the Doctor. 'I can't kill you either.' And he dropped his gun to the ground.

The Dalek couldn't speak for a little while.

'I am the last of the Daleks,' he said at last. His whisper came out as a choked rasp.

'You're not even that,' said the Doctor. 'Rose did more than regenerate you. You're mutating.'

'Into what?'

The Doctor had no answer.

'Rose,' the Dalek said. 'You have contaminated me.' He tried to hate her. He wasn't able to do so.

'I'm sorry,' said the Doctor, and the Dalek clenched in anguish. *I shall not accept this! I do not want the Doctor's pity!* Yes, he did. He wanted the pity of the Doctor.

'But something new,' said Rose. 'Surely that's better?' And she was pleading with him, wanting him to be happy.

'I can feel so much imagination,' the Dalek hissed. 'So much darkness. Rose, I need orders. Give me orders. Order me to die.'

And Rose looked appalled, and the Dalek felt a rush of regret – no, it would not accept regret. No. No. No.

'I can't do that,' she said. 'Please don't ask me to do that.'

'This is not life,' said the Dalek. 'This is sickness. I shall not be like you. I refuse to be like you! Order my destruction.'

And still she wouldn't, and the Dalek felt a fury he hadn't felt in all the years he had been tortured and humiliated. 'Obey!' he screamed. 'Obey! Obey!'

Rose said, 'I order you to die.'

The Dalek fell silent, and it was such a relief to let the fury go.

'I misjudged you,' the Doctor told him.

'No. You judged me correctly. I am a Dalek, and I die to safeguard the purity of the Dalek race.' He would no longer acknowledge the Doctor. The Doctor had failed. The Doctor was beneath the contempt of the Daleks. The Daleks were supreme.

The Dalek felt such a pang of sorrow in Rose's mind, almost like physical pain. He spoke to her softly. 'Are you frightened, Rose Tyler?'

'Yes,' she admitted.

'So am I,' said the Dalek, and he closed his eye, and died.

12

So, the Time War was over, and the Doctor had won.

How about that.

The Doctor stood outside the TARDIS. The old British police box was the most alien of all the alien artefacts in Van Statten's museum. But Van Statten was no longer in any position to appreciate that irony.

The Doctor patted the door with affection. A little piece of home. So long as he had his TARDIS, he wasn't entirely the last remnant of the Time Lords, and he would never be entirely alone.

He wasn't sure if Rose would want to travel with him any longer. They hadn't spoken since the Dalek had died. There hadn't been much time – there had been a lot to do – but even so.

Suddenly, he felt her by his side.

'Are you OK?' she asked.

He wanted to say, *I don't know. I don't know that I can be. But I'm going to try. I really feel I need to try.* What he actually said was, 'Yeah.'

'Good.'

'Are *we* OK? Are we friends?'

'Of course,' said Rose. 'It's just ... different.'

'Different worse?'

'Just different.'

The Doctor nodded, although he wasn't sure he understood.

Then Rose said, 'I'm sorry. All those people who died. And all because of me. I didn't know what I was doing ...'

And he took her in his arms, and she hugged on to him tightly. At last, he let go.

'Rose,' he said. 'Look at me.' So she did. And he saw how much she trusted him still, in spite of everything. 'You were the only one who showed any kindness or compassion. You were the only one who even came *close* to knowing what they were doing.'

Rose squeezed his hand, and smiled.

Adam Mitchell had come to find them. 'We've got to get out of here,' he said. 'Van Statten has disappeared. Goddard says they're closing the base down, like *right now*. I think they're going to fill it with cement. And I'm going to have to go home. To Milton Keynes!'

Rose said, 'Maybe we could give him a lift?'

'Why?' said the Doctor.

'Adam said all his life he wanted to see the stars.'

'Tell him to stand outside, then.'

'He's all on his own, Doctor! And he did help.'

'Rose,' said the Doctor. 'He left you down there.'

'Doctor,' said Rose. 'So did you.'

They glared at each other, and then Rose smiled, and the Doctor did too.

Maybe this is what different is, he thought. *Just for a while.*

'Fine,' he said. 'One trip. But I'm not going to explain the bigger on the inside thing, that's your job.' And he went inside the blue box.

Adam said, 'What are you doing? She said cement. Like, real cement.'

And Rose grinned, and she disappeared inside the blue box too.

'Rose?' called Adam. 'Doctor? What are you doing?'

He looked behind him. In one direction, the threat of cement. In the other, another sort of madness entirely.

He chose the madness, and followed them.

Epilogue

And it ends, as it always has to, with a little boy standing on a hill.

From the top the boy can see the entire world. Fields, check. Trees, check. Lakes, check. The sky above.

And there is no one anywhere, not in any direction, no matter how hard he looks. He is entirely alone.

The little boy is surprised to find himself back there again, to say the least.

But the peace of it. The tranquillity.

The monsters are coming, he thinks.

In his hand he holds a kite, and the kite does the darting and dipping thing that he likes.

The boy loves the pull of the kite in his hands. That it's under his control. That, for once, he's the one giving orders. That, for once, the orders aren't important.

The monsters are coming. But he begins to doubt it. What if they aren't coming? What if he's escaped them all at last?

Is this new life? Or is this death? Or is it neither – is he frozen in a memory, and it's a memory that was never even his?

Does it matter?

From behind the clouds the sun breaks through, and it's warm and it's beautiful and it fills the world.

He knows that soon the kite will come crashing down. And then the sky will come crashing down, and then his life will come crashing down. And then he'll be extinct, and that will be the end of it.

He knows, because everything comes crashing down sooner or later.

But maybe. Just this time. There won't be any monsters.

The little boy reaches up his hand towards the sunlight, and he allows himself a smile, and he has never smiled before.

And he waits to see what will happen next.